THE TETON
BUNCH

Center Point
Large Print

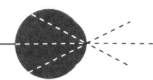

**This Large Print Book carries the
Seal of Approval of N.A.V.H.**

THE TETON BUNCH

— A WESTERN TRIO —

LES SAVAGE, JR.

CENTER POINT LARGE PRINT
THORNDIKE, MAINE

This Circle Ⓥ Western is published by
Center Point Large Print in the year 2017 in
co-operation with Golden West Literary Agency.

Additional copyright material
can be found on page 283.

First Edition
May, 2017

Printed in the United States of America
on permanent paper.
Set in 16-point Times New Roman type.

ISBN: 978-1-68324-384-7

Library of Congress Cataloging-in-Publication Data

Names: Savage, Les, author.
Title: The Teton bunch : a western trio / Les Savage, Jr.
Description: First edition. | Thorndike, Maine : Center Point Large Print,
2017. | Series: A Circle V western
Identifiers: LCCN 2017002074 | ISBN 9781683243847
    (hardcover : alk. paper)
Subjects: LCSH: Western stories. | Large type books.
Classification: LCC PS3569.A826 A6 2017b | DDC 813/.54—dc23
LC record available at https://lccn.loc.gov/2017002074

TABLE OF CONTENTS

TOWN OF TWENTY TRIGGERS

I

Emmet Pierce had seen the trouble coming for some time, now. He leaned indolently against the rear wall of the saloon, a tall man in faded calfskin vest and worn leather ducking breeches. There were a thousand cowhands trailing north from Texas with the same sunburned, rawhide look, the same brush-scarred leggings. Pierce would have been the same as the others but for his gun. It hung low on his long leg, the butt riding high out of leather. It marked him.

His eyes, gleaming strangely in the shadow cast by his gray Stetson, fell on the Joker. That portly, chuckling knave seemed oblivious to the growing tension. He sat back in the rickety chair, black frock coat thrown aside to reveal the fancy flowered waistcoat, stretched tightly across his generous girth. His bland smile was turned on the poker-faced gent across the table, and his little eyes, set deep in fat red cheeks, twinkled with a marvelous innocence.

They had traveled a long way together, Emmet Pierce and the Joker, gathering the stake with which to take over a town. And finally they had hit Benton, wild and lawless, one of a hundred typical boom towns that had sprung up on the Oregon Trail throughout the early 1870s. The west end of Benton's Main Street was a dingy cluster of bawdy houses and cheap hotels and rotgut saloons, false fronts unpainted for the most part, windows broken. The red brick bank and general store and business offices were in the east end. Directly across from the bank was a two-story frame building with a sign stretching the length of its gaudy façade and advertising it as the Poker Palace.

Pierce and the Joker had taken a cheap hotel room. The Joker had spent several days looking around and making a few inquiries. On the third evening, he and Pierce went to the east end, and the portly cardsharp stopped a moment on the plank walk before the big, two-story gambling hall.

"There, Emmet, m' boy, is our spot. I told you we'd take over a town sooner or later, and Benton is the town. We'll start with the Palace. Naturally it doesn't compare with Omaha's Diamond Hall, but it's the best Benton can offer. So tonight the Poker Palace, tomorrow Benton."

Chuckling, he shoved through one of the three sets of batwing doors. The inside was no different than the inside of a hundred other saloons Pierce had seen. He had been born in a saloon. A Texas Ranger had shot down his father in one. And he himself fully expected to die in a saloon. It was the natural gravitating point for men of his kind, men who rode with an eye on their back trail and their guns riding high out of leather.

The Palace had the usual bar at one side, a gilt-edged mirror hanging above, pretzels in a big, cut glass bowl. There were a half dozen card tables in the rear, on either side of a wide stairway that led to a balcony above. The balcony ran across the rear and along each side to the front, doorways opening off it at intervals. The Joker chose one of the tables near the stairs and approached it with his jovial chuckle.

"Room for another, gentlemen?"

Pierce could usually spot the professional gamblers who were in the pay of the house. This one was long and cadaverous in a worn frock coat, sallow face set in a careful mask. His eyes regarded the Joker without enthusiasm.

"You'll need five hundred to sit in. We're playing high stakes."

"Fine, fine." The Joker grinned, drawing up a chair.

So it had started. At first there had been a black-bearded teamster and a pair of townsmen, red and uncomfortable with the look of suckers who were being taken. But the Joker soon forced them out. And now it was a contest between the Poker Palace, and the portly, disarming cardsharp who had magic in his fingers.

Those fingers were working now. It was the Joker's deal. He shoved aside his large pile of gold pieces and chips, and the cards seemed to come to life in his hands. Five cards shot across the

11

table, alighting one on top of the other in front of the other gambler. Eyeing the Joker suspiciously, he took them up, scanned them.

"Two hundred," he bid.

"Oh, come now." The Joker chuckled. "I thought we were playing high stakes. I raise you eight hundred."

A man stood by the stairway, a man with a bullet head that was shaved perfectly clean, and a pair of .45s stuck naked into his broad black belt. Pierce had spotted him at the first. He knew that was where the trouble was coming from.

The house gambler shifted a little in his chair, muttering: "Give me two."

As the Joker sent two cards his way, the man turned his narrow head almost imperceptibly, and his dull eyes slid around until they touched the man with the bullet head, then slid back again, dropping to the new cards.

"Call you," he said.

The bullet-headed man had already begun moving casually over toward the table. Pierce straightened from where he leaned against the wall. Apparently oblivious to the by-play, the Joker put down his four aces and a queen. The other man put his cards face down on the table without speaking.

"Well, well," grinned the Joker, raking in the big pot. "Must be my lucky day."

"You deal yourself some mighty good hands for

a jasper that depends on his luck," said the other.

A small crowd had gathered by now. A few barflies had drifted over; some players from the other tables had quit their game to watch this portly gent clean out the Poker Palace. The bullet-headed man elbowed his way through them, and then he was standing there with his thick legs spread wide, his hammy hands on the butts of his guns.

The house gambler had lost what money he'd won from the townsmen and the teamster. He was playing on the house's chips now, and, patently, he was desperate to recoup his losses. With the deal in his hands, he regained some confidence. He raised the Joker a thousand, and then another. The Joker matched him raise for raise, and the pot grew and grew. It was the gambler who finally stopped it, calling the Joker. There was a marvelous innocence in the Joker's grin as he laid down his cards.

"Well, well, what do you know, a full house," he said.

Pierce had to admire the house gambler a little then. It must have shaken him to lose on his own deal like that. Yet his face remained the sallow mask as he laid his cards down with their faces turned under. But as the Joker began raking in the pot, the gambler turned in that almost imperceptible way, dull eyes sliding to the bullet-headed man. And as the Joker began shuffling the cards through his magic fingers, that man stepped forward, hands still on his guns.

"Wouldn't you like to cash in now, friend?" he asked.

"Why no, not at all." The Joker laughed. "Not at all. The game's just started."

"You don't seem to understand," said the other, and his little eyes took on an ugly glitter. "The boss thinks it's about time you cashed in."

Pierce stepped forward, facing the man across the table. "What's the matter, can't the house back its own deals?"

With a scuffle of feet, the crowd began to fade. The poker-faced gambler shoved back his chair, half rising. The bullet-headed man stepped back, knuckles whitening as his grip on his guns tightened for the draw.

Then the gambler stopped rising, knees still bent. The bullet-headed man's arms jerked as if he were going to draw, but he didn't draw. Pierce's Colt had gotten from its holster into his hand, somehow, and the cocked hammer made a loud sound against the silence. He jerked his head at the gambler.

"Sit back down and take your cards. This game isn't over yet."

Slowly, reluctantly the man eased himself back into his chair. The other took his hands carefully off those naked .45s, and he was still looking at Pierce's gun, as if not yet willing to believe any man could free an iron quite that fast. Through it all, the Joker had sat in his chair, unperturbed. Now he shot five cards to the gambler, chuckling.

"That's it, Emmet, m' boy. I didn't want to cash in so soon as all that."

As the play went on, the gambler began to show the strain despite himself. He wiped sweat from his brow with a swift, impatient swab of his sleeve. He spread his cards between thumb and forefinger, then closed them, then spread them again. And his dull eyes never left the Joker's amazing hands—like a bird fascinated by a snake.

"Two for me," remarked the Joker.

He slipped two cards into the discard pile, then dealt himself a pair, and though Pierce had seen him do it a thousand times before, he couldn't have sworn which cards went where. The crowd had gathered again, and they watched the portly cardsharp's prestidigitations with what approached awe.

The bullet-headed man shifted his feet uncertainly. Perhaps he would have objected to the Joker's mystifying handling of the cards, but he had seen Pierce draw once, and that was enough. The gambler had run out of chips. He was signing chits in a nervous, jerky scrawl.

"Raise you a thousand," said the Joker.

"Call you," answered the gambler, something desperate in his voice.

He made out the chit, then rose, speaking

hoarsely. "All right, ace high, you've broken the bank. You'll have to see the boss."

"I'm downright sorry you want to quit so soon," said the Joker with mock gravity.

He took his time about separating the gold from the chips, unbuttoning his waistcoat, and putting neat stacks of $5 pieces into his money belt. Then he took out a large black wallet and stuffed it with folding money. There were still enough bills left to make a roll that would choke a horse. Finally, he stacked the huge pile of chips, adding them up. He leaned back and said: "With the chips, and those chits you gave me, I make it out that the house owes me twenty-three thousand, five hundred. Want to check?"

The gambler shook his head impatiently, then turned, indicating that they should follow him upstairs. Pierce caught up with the Joker and went up the wide stairway with him, well behind the other man.

"We did it, m' boy," said the Joker, rubbing his hands together. "I told you we'd do big things with my talent and your gun."

A slow grin crossed Pierce's long, sun-darkened face. "Joker, you're the crookedest, dirtiest coyote that ever killed his grandmother for the gold in her teeth, but I have to laugh. I don't think you played one straight hand in that whole game. You even held out aces on him when you passed the cards for his deal."

"Did you spot that?" returned the Joker. "Well, you were acquainted with my methods. They were watching me close. But any time I can't out-prestidigitate two-bit four-flushers like these, I'll take up cattle rustling."

Pierce moved over close and put his hand on the Joker's fat arm, cutting him off. They had climbed the stairs and were walking down the balcony, far enough behind the gambler so he couldn't hear them. But the tread behind them was solid and close. Turning slightly, Pierce saw that the bullet-headed man was following, shaved pate gleaming dully in the overhead light. He grinned inanely at Pierce.

"Never mind," said the Joker, *sotto voce.* "I don't think he knows what prestidigitate means anyway. We're entering the inner sanctum, and I don't think this peace will last much longer. It's your gun more than my talents from here on in, Emmet, m' boy."

Then the gambler was opening the heavy, brass-studded door at the end of the balcony. He ushered them into a large, sumptuous office with pictures of semi-nude women on the walls and the faint odor of expensive whiskey hanging in the air.

Behind the huge mahogany desk sat a heavy man in a loud, checked vest and blue fustian. His beetling black brows met in the center, forming one continuous line above his little eyes, and in one corner of his thick-lipped mouth he held a cold stogie. The strength in his bull-neck and big shoulders was belied by an ineffable weakness in the slack lines of his dissipated face.

"This," said the gambler, "is Mister Dillon."

The Joker kept right on going until he was standing in front of the desk. But Pierce stopped where he could see most of the room. The bullet-headed man must have followed them in, because the door closed with an ominous click.

There was another man standing behind Dillon, back to the window. He wore gray foxed pants and a gray wool vest, and his pair of Paterson five-shots looked too big for his slim, wasp waist. For a moment, his young-old eyes met Pierce's, and there was an instant, tacit under-standing between the men.

"So you're the gazabo who broke my bank?" said Dillon in a rough, surly voice.

The Joker chuckled jovially. He could appear so innocent, so guileless; his round moon face with its plump red cheeks and twinkling eyes had a terribly disarming effect on most men. Pierce could see that effect on Dillon. There had been an uncomfortable question in the big man's eyes, but he relaxed, and a smile broke over his unlovely face.

"I haven't the cash in the house to cover your winnings," he said, reaching for a pen. "You'll take a check, of course."

"Well, now," said the Joker, polishing his ring

against his coat and studying it closely. "I can't say that I will, no. I can't say that I will."

Dillon stopped his hairy hand where it was above the pen. His smile faded. And his chair creaked a little as he leaned back in it.

"Oh," he said. "Oh. You won't take a check."

The boyish figure by the window straightened slightly, one hand slipping down to caress the smooth leather of a holster in an expectant, almost eager way. Pierce took a step sidewise and half turned so that he could see the gambler and the bullet-headed man as well as the others.

The poker-faced cardsharp stood behind a big leather chair to the right of Dillon's desk, his bony hands on its back. The bullet-headed man was standing before the closed door, his thick legs spread apart. He wouldn't have to buck Pierce's draw this time. His .45s were no longer stuck through his belt. They were in his hands, big, potent.

The Joker answered Dillon blandly. "No, I won't take your check. I've been to the bank. I find that you haven't been doing so well, Mister Dillon. I find that your credit doesn't extend as far as my winnings. But what could you expect from a bunch of small timers, anyway?"

Dillon's face reddened, and he took the cold stogie from his mouth. "If you won't take my check, what would you suggest?" he asked sarcastically.

"That you give me and my friend here a half of your business . . . a partnership, shall we say," said the Joker.

For a moment it was completely silent. Dillon's mouth opened a little as if he couldn't quite believe what he'd heard. The man with the bullet head grinned stupidly at Pierce, and Pierce grinned back. He knew he couldn't hope to match those guns. No draw in the world could beat an iron already free. And he knew, too, that Dillon hadn't meant for them to leave alive, no matter what arrangements were reached. Because Dillon was laughing now, a loud, nasty laugh. He turned to the poker-faced gambler behind the chair.

"Hear that, Twoman? He'll let me take him in as a pardner. That fat little four-flusher and his broomstick friend, my pardners. . . ." He stopped, laughing suddenly. "Do you two hicks think you can come in here and break my bank and get away with it? Nobody's ever done anything like that before. I might've let you get out of town if you'd played smart and taken my check. But no, damn you, you had to be stubborn. My pardners . . . hah!"

He looked at the man by the door. "Okay, Bat, I don't want my rug messed up with any blood. Take 'em to the back room."

Bat took a half step forward, but the Joker's voice halted him for an instant—the Joker, who was polishing his ring against his black frock coat, studying it with an unconcerned smile.

"I don't think these gentlemen take us seriously, do you, Emmet?"

"No," said Pierce, and he could feel that old, familiar leap of nerves, that insistent tightening of muscle. "No, I don't think they do. I think we can do right here whatever they wanna do in the back room, can't we, Joker?"

Dillon rose from his chair, almost yelling with rage. "Okay. Okay, Bat, you can get all the blood on my rug you want to!"

Not even Pierce had seen the Joker filch that inkwell from Dillon's desk. Yet, as Bat shifted his .45s to Pierce in a swift, vicious movement, the inkwell hurtled from the portly cardsharp's magic hand, straight into Bat's face, ink spreading out black and blinding all over that bullet head.

Bat staggered backward, howling, firing blindly. But Pierce was already throwing himself at the man's knees, twisting toward the gunman by the window. The slim man with the young-old eyes didn't move from where he was, and his draw was a swift blur of motion, down, up.

Yet Pierce's was swifter. Even as his long, rawhide body crashed into Bat, his gun bellowed.

The heavy slug drove the gunslinger back against the window, smashing the lower pane. He dropped both his guns and slid down to the floor, broken glass spattering over his shoulders.

Before the thunder of his first shot was dead, Pierce was twisting desperately beneath Bat's falling body, and his thumb was carrying back the hammer for a second shot. The gambler had jumped around the chair, a Derringer sliding from his sleeve. He didn't quite have that little gun in his palm when Pierce's Colt slammed again, the shot catching him in the chest.

The gambler flopped back into the chair, weakly trying to raise his weapon. Pierce thumbed out another slug that knocked the man's head back against the leather, making an unrecognizable mess of his poker face.

Bat struggled to his knees, groping for his guns. Pierce rose and slugged him behind his bullet head, and he collapsed without a sound.

The Joker was standing against the wall. He had brought out a Derringer from somewhere on his person, too. It was nickel-plated, double-barreled, deadly. Under its threat, Dillon stood behind his desk, face twisted with a stunned surprise and a growing, impotent anger.

"Now," said the Joker, unperturbed, "we'll draw up the necessary papers for our partnership."

Things had apparently moved too fast for Dillon; his voice came out thick, jerky. "Papers?"

"Why, yes," said the Joker. "Did you think we'd accept your word as a gentleman on the deal?"

II

Emmet Pierce lounged in the big leather chair by Dillon's desk. It was really the Joker's desk now. In the last week since he had broken the bank, the Joker had taken over completely, insinuating himself into control of the Palace with that disarming chuckle and those talented, long-fingered hands, so out of keeping with his portly figure.

The wasp-waisted gunman with the young-old eyes, named Eldon Chiere, had taken Pierce's slug through his chest, high enough above his heart and lungs so that it wasn't fatal. He lay in one of the new rooms that opened off the balcony, his pale face betraying no emotion, neither hate nor pain. Bat had recovered consciousness and in his thick-witted head there seemed no room for enmity. It had simply been a good fight to be enjoyed while it lasted.

The frock-coated gambler, Twoman, was dead. But Pierce had been exonerated at the coroner's inquest, because Twoman had his gun in his hand, and Dillon, under the Joker's genial persuasion, testified that it had been self-defense on Pierce's part.

And now they were on their way to taking over the town. What they would do with it, once they'd taken it over, Pierce couldn't understand. After all, a man could only sit one saddle, only smoke so much, only ride one horse. But Pierce wasn't one to question or worry much. He was glad to stop somewhere. They had ridden such a long trail up from Texas, he and the Joker.

Pierce been born in a little rotgut saloon in Río Hondo, near the Mexican border. His mother had died when he was six. His father had been a drunken, brutal man who mixed in most of the wrong things that went on in that country. His place was a rendezvous for rustlers and smugglers and gunmen on the prod. Pierce had grown up under their influence, never rightly knowing any other kind of men, coming to accept their warped, ruthless code. From that harsh, twisted environment, he formed what moral conceptions he had. And he didn't have many, because his gun usually solved whatever questions arose. Perhaps it was unfortunate that he was so talented with his iron. A man could get into trouble so quickly down by the border when he had that kind of skill. There had been that drunken *hombre* in San Blas when he was fifteen.

Pierce wondered idly if the Rangers were still hunting him for that. The Mexicans called the Rangers *cuerados* because they were clothed and equipped with rawhide. The *cuerado* who shot Pierce's father had come when Pierce was riding with some sticky loop throwers out in the brush. Pierce never knew which crime his father died for, there had been so many of them. He only knew that when he came back and found the elder Pierce, he didn't look very long at the ugly man, lying on the bloodstained floor with fear and pain stamped into his brutal, dead face.

When the Joker came through that part of the country a few months later, with his colorful stories of the opportunities to the north, Pierce was only too glad to ride with him. Pierce had never been one to follow his trail with another man, and he told himself he could part company with the portly, amusing scoundrel whenever he wished. Perhaps it was that he had ridden alone too long, or perhaps it was the attraction of opposite personalities. Whatever it was, they never parted. They rode north, through Oklahoma and the Kansas cow towns, Abilene, Dodge City, Wichita. The Joker took care of their finances with his amazing fingers and his intimate knowledge of all games of chance, and Pierce took care of their skins with his iron.

The Joker had always looked for a town to take over. He had great plans for what they could do together, with his talents and Pierce's skill. He said the cow towns were already too much in the control of the powerful cattle interests; and when they hit the Missouri, he claimed the towns like Westport and St. Joe were too stodgy and settled and law-abiding. Then they hit the Oregon Trail, Omaha, Scottsbluff, Laramie, and finally Benton.

"This, m' boy," said the Joker, "is the town. No law to speak of. Enough suckers to last me a lifetime. Wild men and wild women and money to be made by the clever *hombres*. You and I, m' boy, are taking over."

And so they were. Already Pierce had started gathering trigger men around him. From where he sat in the comfortable armchair, he could see Georgie Nix leaning on the balcony rail and watching the floor below. A big, solid, black-haired man, Nix, with white teeth and a handsome face. He had been pushed north from Texas by the same things that pushed Pierce, the things that were inevitably behind men of their kind. The carefully kept look to his well-oiled, double action .45 stamped him and his skill. And he did have a deadly swift skill, for all his bulk. Pierce had seen it more than once.

Al McGowan was another. Pierce had found him shooting up the Dancing Lady Saloon in Benton's tough west end. He had been a short little figure in worn Justins, gun belt buckled around the outside of a thick Mackinaw. He had been pie-eyed, soaked to the gills, as roaring drunk as any man Pierce had ever seen. Yet he had stood in the middle of the floor, with a big .44 in each hand, and every shot he triggered out found a target. So Pierce hired him.

There were others—Tom Farril, Hanson, Carter—godless men without consciences, men whose only loyalty was to the money they made with their guns. Pierce didn't think of them particularly as badmen. He had lived among them too long for that.

The Joker's voice cut through his thoughts. He could see the portly gent coming down the balcony with a tall, mournful-looking man in a dusty black fustian and flat-crowned Stetson, a carpetbag in one bony hand. The Joker was sporting a new frock coat and fancy-topped Hyer boots. A sizable diamond had replaced the smaller ring. He said hello to Georgie Nix and entered the room, polishing the sparkler against his coat.

"Emmet, m' boy, I want you to meet Gentleman George, an old crony of mine. We ran a bunko game in New Orleans once."

Pierce rose, shaking hands with Gentleman George. The Joker plumped himself in the swivel chair behind the desk, leaning back and taking an expensive cigar from his breast pocket.

"Emmet, it's about time we started going to work for good. The town council is sitting on some weighty matters in a few days. Seems like Benton's been getting a little too wild for them . . . they're going to crack down on such establishments as the Poker Palace. I don't know exactly what they have in mind, but I thought it was about time to show them who's boss. In nosing around, I find that the winter of 'Sixty-Seven was a rather hard one. Hit most of the cattlemen below the belt. Clem Albright's bank holds mortgages on most of the cow outfits in the vicinity. Keeth Albright and Pete Wells and a jasper named Rickett all sit on the city council. They're pretty big cowmen, and their three votes have more weight than all the others put together. If we controlled them, we'd control the council. So, Gentleman George here is going to start a run on the bank."

"Is there a connection?" asked Pierce.

The Joker chuckled indulgently. "Good old single-track Emmet, never more than one idea at a time. But then that's your value, isn't it? Get you set on a road, and all hell and high water can't get you off till you reach the end. Of course there's a connection. Gentleman George is going to the best hotel in Benton and register as the bank examiner. He's just hit town. Nobody knows him. He'll let it out, very discreetly of course, that the bank is not quite as solvent as it should be, and that he's been sent up to check the books. As soon as the rumor spreads far enough, you'll see the connection between Rickett and Wells and a run on Albright's bank."

Pierce grinned, shrugged. He had never claimed too many brains anyway. He didn't mind the Joker riding him like that, as long as he did it with his cheerful laugh.

"Take the gentleman down to Elm House,

Emmet, and sort of drop the hint here and there that he's the bank examiner. Then you come back and watch this little burg go into the biggest bobble it's ever had."

Pierce led the mournful man out and down the stairs. The Palace had changed under the Joker's amazing hand. There was a big, green-topped roulette table up front with a tall, black-coated croupier calling out the numbers in a monotonous tone. The number of bartenders had doubled; half a dozen of the Joker's old acquaintances had wandered in from various places on the back trail, bunko artists and cardsharps and Missouri river gamblers. They lounged around the rear tables, taking care of the suckers and the townsmen with a systematic, crooked efficiency that only the Joker could have organized. Pierce was passing the bar when a young man stepped out in front, stopping him.

"You're Mister Pierce, aren't you?"

He was no more than a kid, really, in old boots and worn Levi's, a hank of dark hair falling over his smooth young forehead. There was a look shining in his eyes that Pierce knew well enough. That same look must have been in his own eyes at this boy's age, when the swashbuckling gunnies had come into that saloon down in Río Hondo.

He said uncomfortably: "Yes, I'm Pierce."

"You're hiring men," said the boy. "I'd like to sign on."

Pierce looked at the boy's gun. It had a new, unused look, and the holster was stiff and shiny, and it seemed very pathetic. Pierce's voice was unnaturally gruff.

"You go home, kid. You take that gun back to the store and go home."

A hurt look mingled with the awed shine in the boy's eyes. "But I've been practicing. Give me a chance, Mister Pierce. . . ."

It was then that the girl came through the batwing doors. She stopped an instant, perhaps dazzled a little by the bizarre crowds shifting around the roulette table and all the cut glass that was piled in glimmering stacks on the bar. Then she saw the boy and Pierce, and she walked decisively toward them, an angry tilt to her chin.

"Jerry Albright, I told you not to come here," she said hotly. "Now you turn right around and go out and help load Uncle Keeth's hay in his wagon. And give me that gun."

"Lisa," began the boy, flushing. "You leave me alone. . . ."

"Give it to me," she said, holding out a little hand, tanned by the sun, ignoring Pierce and Gentleman George.

Tears of impotent anger were in the boy's eyes as he unbuckled the belt and handed the gun to her. As he stamped toward the doors, she turned to Pierce. Anger still flashed in her dark eyes. Her lustrous brown hair framed a face that would be beautiful when it matured. Now there was a certain strength beneath its smooth, girlish lines, a stubborn quality to her rather full-lipped mouth. She wore a buckskin vest over her flannel shirt, and her small worn boots, beneath the leather skirt, were run over at the heels, looking as if she did more walking than riding.

Pierce had time to take it all in because she stood there, looking at him for a long moment without speaking. Finally he had to say something to cover his own embarrassment. "You must be Clem Albright's girl. I've seen you around town."

She didn't smile. "They say you killed a man in here last week. You don't look like it bothered you much."

He turned to the crowd at the front table. "See all them *hombres*, ma'am. There probably isn't a one of 'em that hasn't used his gun on a man, sometime."

"That's different," she said. "They aren't paid to do their killing."

"Nobody pays me," he said.

She spoke impatiently. "This new gambler who's taken over the Palace . . . they say you're his man."

"I'm nobody's man," he said. "The Joker and me are partners. I never took money for my gun, I never will."

A delicate flush crept into her face and she stamped her foot. "You're a gunman all the same,

31

and if you don't leave my brother alone, I'll take this Forty-Five to you myself!"

She turned on her heel and walked toward the batwings, boots making a small, angry pound. Pierce watched her go, wondering why the hell he should have bothered to explain anything to a girl. He'd never tried to justify himself before to anyone, not even himself.

Dillon's voice cut off his thoughts. "Well, looks like you got an admirer."

Pierce turned to see the man, standing at the bar, eyes bleary with drink, dead cigar stuck into one side of his mouth.

"Dillon," said Pierce. "You keep your opinions to yourself or the Joker is liable to lose one of his partners."

As usual, the Joker played his cards with incredible results. It took but one day for the rumor to get around that the bank's books were being examined. In this wild, new country, few men had had many dealings with banks, and Benton was ripe for what the Joker was perpetrating. The day after Gentleman George registered at the Elm House, the run began on Clem Albright's red brick bank at the east end of Main. Pierce and the Joker stood at the window of the Palace's office and watched the crowd grow in the street below.

"Look at 'em, Emmet, m' boy . . . suckers." The Joker chuckled. "The majority of the world is suckers, Emmet, born to be bilked. I wouldn't be happy without 'em. Know something funny? I thought you were a sucker when I first spotted you down there in Río Hondo. You're deceptive, Emmet, you play your cards close to your vest. I don't think I could put much over on you, could I?"

"You haven't tried yet, Joker," said Pierce, sniffing at the other's pungent cigar smoke. "Seems that stogie's something new with you, isn't it?"

The portly gambler turned, grinning. "A mark of my station. I'm a big shot now, y'know. New clothes, new boots, cigars. They all fit in. I tell you, we're slated to be the biggest men in this country. You should get a new outfit, new gun. Dress to suit the job, Emmet. You're my right-hand man, y'know."

"Oh, I thought I was your partner," said Pierce. "Anyway, you know I wouldn't get another gun. And as to my clothes, it took a long time to get them comfortable. I don't want to start in all over again."

Dillon came into the room, face flushed with drink, voice thick. "Clem Albright's comin' up, just like you said he would, Joker."

The Joker had been smiling affably at Pierce. He turned to Dillon, and though that smile still wreathed his plump face, it had suddenly lost all its mirth; it had taken on an ineffable quality of cold, deadly menace.

"Dillon," said the portly man, and his voice was

strangely flat. "If there is anything I despise more than a weak man, it's a man who can't hold his liquor. Sit down and keep your mouth shut."

Dillon paled, lurching into the chair on the other side of the desk. He wasn't the same man who had ordered Bat to kill the Joker and Pierce in that harsh, confident voice such a short time ago. For the first few days, the Joker had let him think he had as much say-so as before, deferring to his judgment, asking his advice. But slowly, subtly, cleverly the Joker had taken over, until Dillon's partnership consisted of no more than his name on the paper he had signed.

All of Dillon's arrogance and strength had been built on his concrete possessions, on the Poker Palace. As he became aware that everything was slipping from beneath him, and that he was helpless against the Joker's sly machinations, he began to crack. Pierce wondered how much longer there would be three partners in the Poker Palace.

Clem Albright came hurrying down the hall and into the room. He was a short, confused-looking little man with a fringe of gray hair encircling a shining pate, and steel-rimmed glasses. He wiped a perspiring hand against his drab coat and stopped before the desk, looking about him hesitantly, finally focusing his myopic gaze on the Joker.

"Well, well," said the portly gambler. "Mister

Albright. What can I do for you, sir, what can I do for you?"

"I won't mince words, Mister Joker," said Albright, leaning forward, almost pleading. "For some reason there's a run on my bank. I can't understand it. We're normally solvent. Last winter was bad, of course, and a lot of cattlemen borrowed from us. But the whole town is down there, demanding every penny they've put in, and I've heard that outlying ranchers are coming to withdraw their funds, too."

Pierce could hear the dull hubbub of the crowd down below, growing louder every moment. Albright's face grew pale. The Joker shrugged.

"Why come to me, Albright?"

"The Palace hasn't banked any money since the day you took over," said Albright. "I know you have enough in the house to help me, Mister Joker, and you've got to help me. I'll be ruined unless I can pay them off, and if they see I'm solvent, they'll start depositing again."

The portly gambler shot Pierce a sly look, then turned his disarming smile on Albright. "Well, I'll see what I can do. But I'll need some security. Say the mortgages you hold."

"Yes," said Albright doubtfully, "I think I could give you one or two mortgages for security."

"Not one or two, Mister Albright," said the Joker. "All of them."

Albright took his hands from the desk and his

small mouth worked a moment before the words came out. "All . . . all . . . of them. But our bank holds over two dozen. We've loaned almost every cattleman around here the money to get back on his feet after that winter of 'Sixty-Seven. Surely, you're not serious."

The Joker hoisted himself from his swivel chair and his bland, cheerful smile held the confidence of a man who holds all the aces. "Those are my terms, Albright. If you don't care to meet them, that's your business, isn't it?"

"B-b-but this is mad . . . ," stumbled the banker.

The Joker turned and stepped to the window. The noise of the crowd drifted up, and the expression on the portly man's fat face as he looked down was eloquent. Finally, Albright said heavily: "All right. There's nothing else I can do. I'll have the mortgages here in fifteen minutes."

He turned and walked out, a small, harmless figure, pitiful in his confusion and misery. The Joker turned back then, chuckling until his big belly quivered beneath the fancy new waistcoat. "Now, Emmet, do you understand the connection between Gentleman George, and Rickett and Wells and Keeth Albright. With their mortgages in my hands, I'm sure they won't be so eager to clean up the town, will they?"

Pierce rose from the leather armchair, moving toward the door. What was there about Clem

Albright's beaten, pathetic figure that made him feel strangely nauseated? He had seen the Joker fleece countless other suckers before, and hadn't thought much one way or the other about it. Could it be because Albright was the girl's father? Pierce had thought about Lisa more than once since their meeting. Or perhaps he, too, had been disarmed by the Joker's affable chuckle, perhaps he hadn't realized just how much he had fallen under the Joker's influence. That could happen. The Joker was so subtle and sly and charming. Pierce wished, somehow, that they had never started this thing.

III

Willard Rickett was a tall man in his late forties, large mouth and open face revealing his frank, guileless nature. He stood before the Joker's desk, anger in his eyes as well as an unease, plaid Mackinaw and barrel-leg chaps dusty with the long ride from his spread. Peter Wells was corporal of the Lazy H. He was the same type as Rickett, honest, straightforward, totally incapable of coping with the Joker's devious, nimble, crooked way of doing things. The only man who seemed to approach an understanding of the Joker's capabilities was Keeth Albright, Clem's brother. The moment he had entered the office, his piercing blue eyes had settled on the beaming Joker in a speculative, studying way.

He was a lanky, broad-shouldered man, Albright, iron-gray hair and strong, hawk-like nose giving him distinction, chaps and buffalo coat as dusty as the clothes of the other two men. His assumption of leadership was immediate and unconscious.

"All right, Joker," he said, "let's have it. I don't know why the hell you sent Pierce after me and the others. I wouldn't have come for any other man."

His steely eyes moved to Pierce, and for a moment there was a flitting admiration in them, the admiration of one strong man who recognizes strength in another. Then he turned back to the Joker. The gambler sat tilted back in his chair, smiling, eyes wrinkling, his whole attitude so innocent that Pierce had to smile faintly.

"Albright," said the Joker. "You're the kind of a man who takes his coffin varnish straight from the bottle, so that's the way I'll give it to you. Next week the city council is sitting . . ."

"That's right," interrupted Albright. "And before we're through, the Poker Palace will be closed and you'll be on your way, Mister Joker, along with all your gunmen and your crooked tables and your watered whiskey. We'll put you in tar and feathers and we'll ride you down Main Street on a rail ripped from this very building. So now, go on."

Joker was unperturbed. "That's why I called you

in here, Albright. I don't think you're going to pass any legislation along the lines you've just mentioned, no, I don't think you are. You and your two friends, here, bear enough weight in the council to swing opinion one way or the other. When any motion comes up that would be harmful to my interests, you'll see that it's squelched."

"What," flamed Rickett. "Are you loco . . . ?"

"He's got something up his sleeve, Will, can't you see that?" snapped Albright, stepping forward until his flat belly was jammed against the desk. "And it had better be good, Joker!"

"It is good, gentlemen, it is good," said the Joker. "I hold your mortgages."

Impatience was in Wells's voice. "The last I heard of 'em they was in Clem Albright's bank vault."

"No more," said the Joker, pulling himself out of the chair.

Big black-haired Georgie Nix stood by the safe. He stepped away, allowing the Joker to open it, fumble around on the top shelf, and draw out two official-looking sheaves. For a long moment, Rickett and Wells stared at their mortgages. Defeat showed in the deepening of lines about Rickett's wide, generous mouth. Peter Wells rubbed a dazed hand across his chin.

"It would be unfortunate, wouldn't it, if I were forced to foreclose on you gentlemen?" said the Joker softly. "Your terms are up soon, you know. I

39

imagine you've just about wrapped your whole lives around your outfits. I'm sure you see things my way now."

"Yeah," said Rickett dully. "I reckon you got us acrost a barrel, Joker."

"Fine, fine," said the Joker. "I'm glad you're such intelligent men. Oh, yes, there's one other thing. As long as the council's sitting, I want you to propose a ten-thousand-dollar operating fee on all establishments serving liquor or running a gambling game of any sort."

Wells frowned. "You know those tinhorn saloons down in the west end couldn't raise ten thousand dollars in ten thousand years. You'll be the only one able to pay it."

"Correct," said the Joker dryly. "Absolutely correct. And when the town marshal has closed all the saloons in the west end, that will give the Poker Palace what is known as a monopoly, won't it?"

Rickett snorted in disgust. "If you ain't the dirtiest, orneriest coyote this side of hell."

He turned on his heel and stalked out, Wells following. They had brought some waddies with them, taciturn, suspicious young men, hard and sunburned. The little group made a lot of noise going down the balcony, spurs dragging, chains rattling, leather creaking. The Joker called after them.

"If your marshal needs any help closing those

saloons, let me know and I'll send some of the boys along with him."

Albright whirled after his friends. "Wait a minute, Wells. You can't let him take you this way. You can't just lie down under his boots. Where the hell's your guts?"

Wells turned slowly at the corner of the balcony, eyes dull, shoulders stooped in defeat. "You can talk that way, Keeth. He hasn't got any mortgage of yours. And what would you do if he had one?"

Albright had no answer for that. He was a cattle-man. He would know how much their spreads meant to them, how long and painfully they had slaved for what they now owned. He would understand how a man could come to love the sweet smell of the hip-high bluestem in the spring, how the plaintive bawl of cattle from some bottom land could enter a man's heart. Finally, he turned back to the Joker. "Why the hell did you call me up? You can't control me with any mortgage. I didn't go to my brother for help last winter, thank God."

The Joker smiled. "You wouldn't want me to foreclose on your friends, Albright, would you? But if you won't string along, well . . ."

Albright bellied up against the desk again and his big strong, rope-scarred hands were spread out flat on the top, his piercing eyes bored into the Joker's. "You wouldn't foreclose on Wells or Rickett if I didn't fall in line. Because if you did

41

foreclose, you'd lose your hold on them, and you'd be right back where you started. That's the only value in those mortgages for you . . . the hold they give you. So you can't rope me into your dirty game, Joker, you haven't got anything to do it with."

"There are other ways than . . . mortgages," said the Joker, and he never seemed more amiable than now. "Your brother's bank is in a bad way. Soon I'll be in a position to make him or break him. What I do is up to you, tonight."

"I'm sure my brother'd rather close his doors than kowtow to a fat, conniving polecat like you," said Albright tensely. "I know I'm speaking for him when I tell you to go to hell!"

He turned on his heel and walked out, a tall, strong man with an uncompromising look to his broad shoulders. The Joker put his elbows on the desk and placed his fingers together, studying them with a singularly evil grin. "Well," he said. "It seems I underestimate Mister Keeth Albright. I'll have to think up something specially excruciating for him. I've discovered within me a sudden intense desire to see him squirm."

Pierce rolled himself a cigarette, studying the Joker. The gambler had grown fatter in the last weeks. He left the bottom of his waistcoat unbuttoned. He didn't get outdoors much any more, either, and his cheeks were no longer red and jolly. Their sallow puffiness had taken on a look of unhealthiness that was at times almost revolting.

"The west end's Arvin Kane's district," said Pierce. "He won't like you moving in on him that way."

The Joker took out an expensive Rialto, bit off the end. "Did you think I'd stop at the Poker Palace? I told you we're taking over this whole town, end to end, all the buildings and the business and the suckers. I suppose I could have just sent you and the boys down to wipe out Kane and his mob of toughs. But why do it the hard way? Besides, it was as good a time as any to see just how the council reacts. And after I've talked with Marshal Torrance, I'm sure he won't collect the ten-thousand-dollar tax from me." He went back to the safe, putting the mortgages away, taking out a cashbox. "Your split for the week is twenty thousand, Emmet, m' boy. That's out of the net profits, of course."

Pierce shrugged, smiling dryly. "I'll need thirty dollars. Feed bill I owe on my horse and some tobacco. Keep the rest for me."

"That's right. If you put all the money you already made in Clem Albright's bank, he'd have enough to pay me back. That would be ironical, being paid back with my own money wouldn't it?" The Joker chuckled. "Besides, I want to keep these mortgages. It might come in handy to have a bank around someday."

His chuckle grew until his paunch quivered, and the big gold watch chain across his waistcoat bobbed up and down. Pierce turned back to the window, strangely irritated. That's what he had liked about the Joker from the first, his perpetual humor, his ever-ready laugh. Pierce wondered why it should gall him now.

The marshal picked Saturday to close the saloons. It was the middle of summer, and a heavy, stifling humidity accompanied the afternoon heat. A large crowd had sought the diversions offered by the Palace by the time Pierce led his three gunmen down the stairs and through the lower hall. There were three big tables in front now, instead of one. Roulette and monte and faro each drew their crowds of devotees. The Joker had put in huge glittering chandeliers that reflected the light of ornate oil lamps, set around the walls that were themselves hung with rich velvet and shimmering folds of silk. Thick red carpets covered the approach to the stairs, and the stairway, and potted plants stood in gilded vases on either side of each set of batwing doors. Chiere and McGowan and Nix followed Pierce through it all without much interest. They were too intimately acquainted with the shining display to be impressed any more.

The blazing sunlight hit Pierce in the face as he stepped outside, blinding him momentarily. He turned to the marshal's office next door to the Palace, a big frame building that had been converted from a barn, holding the town's jail in its rear.

The Saturday night crowds were already gathering. A bunch of cowhands with Lazy H brands on their mule-hocked ponies came galloping down the street, whooping and yelling. A long train of freight wagons creaked toward the Russell, Majors & Waddell agency at the other end of Main. The teamsters cast impatient looks at the saloons, licking dry lips. It was a poor time, Pierce reflected, to be closing those rotgut saloons of Kane's. They would be crowded with all the toughs in from the trail and all the wild cowhands, and the townsmen out for their weekly spree.

Charlie Torrance was the marshal, a bandy-legged, pot-bellied man with a drooping, untidy mustache and a certain sly shiftiness to his watery blue eyes that might have meant he was the kind of gent who drifted whichever way the wind blew. He came up from the cell-block when he saw Pierce's tall figure in the doorway. "The Joker said he'd send some of you boys down. Don't think I could've done much toward closing Kane up by myself. He's a tough *hombre*."

Pierce said: "Let's go."

He turned to walk back out. Eldon Chiere lounged just inside the door, gray pants tucked into plain half-boots, Paterson Colts still too big for his wasp waist. His dead eyes were regarding Pierce fixedly, his face a pale mask. Pierce had the sudden, unreasonable feeling that Chiere had watched him like that ever since they left the Joker's office. It made him feel cold inside. The wasp-waisted gunman had never evidenced any hatred toward Pierce for putting that hunk of .45 lead through his narrow chest up there in Dillon's office so many weeks ago. But then he never showed any emotion anyway. He might have a consuming hatred for Pierce, and nobody would ever suspect it. Pierce moved out on the sidewalk, allowing Chiere to catch up with him. That way he could watch the man's hands.

As they neared the west end, the crowd thickened. A drunk cowpuncher lurched into Pierce, looked up with bleary eyes to see who he had bumped. A sudden recognition came into his face and he jerked away quickly. A pair of thick-chested muleskinners stepped off the walk to let Pierce and his party by.

"Look how they let you through . . . like you was king or something," cackled Torrance. "By damn if you ain't got a rep already."

Pierce shrugged, lips thinning. He had never sought a rep with his gun. It was just something he used when he needed it.

They were directly across the street from the white frame boarding house that Clem Albright owned and now lived in. Jerry Albright was on the porch. He must have spotted Pierce easily, for the Texan towered above most of the crowd, a tall long-faced man in that faded calfskin vest with grease spots showing on the front where he had wiped his fingers when he was on the trail and had no better napkin. The boy clattered down the steps, dodged around a big Conestoga wagon, ducked under a hitch rack.

"Can I go with you today, Mister Pierce? I got my gun back. If you're gonna close Kane's saloons, you might need another man."

Pierce stopped. "How'd you know we were going to close the saloons?"

The boy flushed, didn't answer. Georgie Nix's voice was a gruff mutter in Pierce's ear.

"Keeth Albright's the kid's uncle, y'know. He's been shootin' off his mouth all around town about you and the Joker. Everybody knows the Joker's behind that tax on the saloons."

Pierce's face tightened a little. "I told you once to go home, kid. Now get the hell out."

He turned away and broke into a swift walk, feeling rotten, boots a sharp, angry sound on the sidewalk. The others had to half run to keep up with his long-legged stride. They passed the Emery Hostelry where he stabled his horse, and the ramshackle rooming house where he and the Joker had first stayed. Arvin Kane's Dancing Lady sported a battered overhang that sagged forlornly, and a pair of big windows, panes long broken by some drunken revelers. The batwing doors creaked as Pierce shoved through them into the dimly lighted room with its trio of rickety deal tables, its warped flooring. Kane came around from behind the ancient bar when he saw Pierce.

He was a short, heavy-set man with a beer belly shoving at his soiled waistcoat. His greasy, unshaven chin took on a stubborn jut and his little eyes flamed angrily. For all his seedy, run-down look, there was a certain strength to the way he took his stand, short legs spread wide, hammy hands on his broad hips. "Well, Pierce," he snarled. "So they had to send you and your boys along with the marshal. I think you'll find this end of town don't welcome the Joker's men."

Torrance cast an oblique glance at Pierce as if for assurance. "I was in yesterday to collect that tax, Kane, and I told you I'd close you up if you couldn't pay it. Git your patrons moving."

Kane still spoke to Pierce. "I know who's behind this. The Joker wants to take over the west end just like he took over the Poker Palace. If you think you and your two-bit triggermen can do anything down here, just try it, Pierce, just try it."

Pierce swept the room with a swift glance. A rough, ugly man with the look of a bouncer in his heavy shoulders and a cauliflower ear had moved in behind Kane. He had a big Bowie stuck into his belt. A pair of narrow-faced gunnies had risen from one of the card tables, nervous, waiting. Other toughs were grinning, gathering.

Pierce knew he didn't have to speak to his own men. He had chosen them for this very thing, and they would back him well enough. He took a step forward, speaking to the men at the bar, at the tables. "Mister Kane hasn't been able to pay his operating tax, gentlemen, and the marshal is closing his doors. So if you'll move out in a quiet, orderly fashion, it'll save a lot of trouble."

There was a man by the bar wearing a big white sombrero who began to laugh in a harsh, loud way. Pierce's thundering shot cut that laugh off, and the sombrero jerked off the man's head, plopping to the floor, a neat, round puncture in its white crown where the bullet had entered.

"Now," said Pierce. "Will you move out in a quiet, orderly fashion?"

Kane half turned, looking at his bouncer, at the gunnies by the card table, at the toughs near the bar. The bouncer's eyes were glued to Pierce's gun, and his ugly mouth sagged a little. One of the gunmen licked dry lips, hand moving upward and away from his iron. The man who laughed seemed to be swallowing, his Adam's apple moving up and down jerkily. Slowly Kane comprehended, and a dark red flush swept his unshaven cheeks. His voice came out thick with impotent anger.

"Well, you damned yellow-bellied prairie lawyers, are you gonna stand there and let this broomstick triggerman take over the whole west end?" He turned to his gunmen. "Slap your leather, damn you. What the hell d'ya think I hire you for? Pierce has three men and we have a dozen and you stand there and let him tell you where to get off. . . ."

He broke off, choked with his own anger, turning viciously from side to side. Finally he whirled to Pierce, almost yelling. "All right, damn you, all right! You got this hand. But you can go back and tell that fat little Joker, he don't know what he's started. The Dancing Lady isn't all of the west end by a long shot, and if he thinks he can take me over without a fight, he's in for a big surprise. Go ahead and close my doors, close all of 'em. They won't stay that way long!"

He turned on his heel, shoving his bouncer violently out of the way and stalking through a rear door. Pierce jerked his head toward the crowd, emphasizing his desires with a wave of his still-smoking Colt. Slowly, nervously the men began to move away from the bar and eddy around him, heading for the door.

"Okay, Torrance," said Pierce. "You can close up and post your notices."

"I'll get a couple of deputies to nail some boards across those batwings," said the marshal. "I would've brought 'em along, but . . ."

"But you didn't think we could do the job," supplied Pierce.

"I guess that's right." Torrance nodded. "Everybody said the Joker was the man to look out for. You stood around so quiet, I didn't realize what kind of an *hombre* you really were. I think people are wrong about the Joker. I think you're a helluva lot more dangerous than him."

"Come on," said Pierce. "We've got some more saloons to close."

IV

Emmet Pierce walked down the thickly carpeted balcony toward the Joker's office. It was all over now. Word had passed swiftly through the west end of what had happened in the Dancing Lady, and there was no trouble about closing the other saloons. Torrance's deputies had nailed planks across the batwings, and when Pierce had left, that end of Main Street had been filled from sidewalk to sidewalk with the sullen, dangerous crowd of men who had been ejected from their haunts.

There was always a man lounging on the balcony rail just outside the office, keeping an eye on the lower hall, a .30-30 Winchester leaning by his side. Tom Farril was there now, six-foot-three of Oklahoma gunslick, a taciturn, deadly man in old barrel-leg chaps and patched flannel shirt. He turned an Indian-dark, sloe-eyed face to Pierce, nodding an indifferent greeting.

The office door was ajar. Nix and McGowan had stayed below, but Eldon Chiere was behind Pierce, and he followed him into the room. Pierce stopped just inside the door. His face might have tightened a little, but it didn't show the surprise he felt. Jerry Albright stood near the big black safe. His eyes had that hesitant, hopeful look, and that awe. Pierce didn't try to keep the anger from his voice.

"What're you doing here, kid?"

The Joker answered for the boy. "Meet our new triggerman, Emmet. I want you to show him the ropes."

Pierce hadn't yet looked at the portly gambler; his eyes were still hard on Albright. "Go on outside, kid. I'd like to talk with the Joker."

The boy moved through the door sideways, a plea in his face. Pierce watched him until he turned into the last of the rooms that led off the balcony, where the men bunked. Then he shut the heavy, brass-studded door and turned to face the Joker, a controlled anger in his compressed lips. "When'd you hire him?"

The Joker grinned. "Half an hour ago. He admires you no end, Emmet, m' boy. I guess kids are that way. See a man with a talent and a certain rep, and they make a little tin god out of him. I remember I used to worship a bunko artist in

Saint Louis when I was about ten. I told you I'd find something especially excruciating for Keeth Albright."

"You can't haul that kid into your dirty game, Joker," said Pierce flatly. "He doesn't belong. He's clean and right, not our kind."

The Joker's grin faded momentarily, then grew again. He leaned back and put the tips of his fingers together, studying them. Chiere had moved around until he stood with his back to the window. Pierce remembered the last time he had stood that way.

"Emmet," said the Joker, pursing his lips, "you don't seem to realize what a hold over Keeth Albright this kid gives us. Ironically enough, Jerry admires you much more than he does his uncle. The kid's almost twenty. I don't think Clem, or that filly, or Keeth could make him quit here now. And I think Keeth will step a little easier, with his nephew right in our very midst, so to speak, don't you?"

Pierce's voice had softened until it seemed to have lost most of its anger. "I've always handled your triggermen, Joker, and I'm firing Jerry Albright."

The Joker still smiled. But all the mirth gone, leaving something cold, something ineffably deadly. His eyes lost their twinkle, receding into fat cheeks. When he spoke, it was between heavy breaths.

"I've seen this coming for a long time, Emmet, m' boy, and I haven't liked it. Most men underestimate you because you're so damned quiet and unassuming. But I've been with you too long to do any underestimating. It isn't just because you pack a gun and have a certain talent with it, Emmet. You'd be the same kind of *hombre* without an iron. Bucking you is like drawing to an inside straight. A man's a fool to do it. And I'm no fool, Emmet, I guess you know that. But this was inevitable, wasn't it?" He looked up suddenly, and a little pulse Pierce had never noticed before was beating in his pale forehead. "You're not firing the kid," he said.

Pierce felt a sudden quickening of his breath, that familiar tightening of muscle and tingling of nerves. His eyes went past the Joker to Chiere, who had straightened suddenly. His young-old eyes met Pierce's, and there was that same, instant tacit understanding. It had been so much like this before, only Dillon had sat at the desk, and Bat had stood at the door.

Yes, the Joker had seen it coming for a long time. And he had prepared for it. Chiere would be a good successor to Pierce. He had fewer scruples.

"Did you hear me, Emmet?" said the Joker, with that cold smile. "I said you aren't going to fire the kid."

Pierce set himself like he had done so many times before, because he saw that's how it was going to be. Chiere was waiting, and this time he knew Pierce's skill. The Joker was waiting, and though he had never been a gunman, he carried that Derringer somewhere about his person. Pierce knew he couldn't get both men at once. His fingers curled instinctively as he opened his mouth to speak.

He didn't get the words out. Someone burst through the door, crying out in a frightened, feminine voice: "Where's my brother? I know he's here. You've got to get him out before they come. Please, where is he?"

Pierce turned to Lisa Albright. Her face was flushed and the beauty of its fear and excitement struck at him sharply. He grabbed her soft young arm, asking: "Get your brother out before who comes?"

She drew away. "Kane and his crowd. They're coming to wreck this place because the Joker closed those saloons, they're coming to wipe you out, the biggest crowd I've ever seen in Benton!"

Even before she stopped speaking, Pierce became aware of the dull, growing mutter outside. He turned to the Joker. The portly gambler had risen and stepped to the open window.

The oil lamps hadn't been turned on yet, and the late afternoon sunlight cast a weird glow over the Joker. He looked like some strange gargoyle, leaning over the sill, shoulders hunched, fore-shortened head only a round knob with three distinct wrinkles in the back of his fat neck just above the collar.

"She's right," he said. "I can see Kane in front. I didn't think there were that many men in Benton."

Lisa grabbed Pierce, almost screaming. "Where's my brother? He doesn't have anything to do with this. You've got to get him out."

The Joker turned. "It's too late to get anybody out. They're almost at our doors. Get your trigger-men, Pierce. It's what you picked them for. It's your job."

He seemed to have forgotten the death that had stood between them a moment before. And suddenly Pierce forgot it, too. This wasn't any of the dirty, underhanded games the Joker played. This was a fight, his kind of a fight. Pierce felt a sudden, unnamable release as he took a long step past the girl, throwing his words back over his shoulder. "Lisa, you stay right here. I'm sending Nix up with a scatter-gun to guard the safe, and it'll be the best place."

He was running when he passed Farril. He didn't even speak to the Oklahoman; he knew he didn't have to. Farril would make his slugs count. He pounded around the corner of the balcony and ran to the head of the wide, richly carpeted stairway that led down into the center of the hall. He made a tall, commanding figure there on the top step, gray Stetson cuffed far enough back to let the light fall on his harsh-planed face. His deep Texas drawl carried above the hubbub of the crowd below.

"Arvin Kane's coming with his crew from the west end. I want this whole damned crowd out the back way right now! You croupiers, get 'em moving, get 'em out the back doors, clear the floor. Nix, get a scatter-gun from the bar and leg it to the Joker's office. You know what to do if any of Kane's men get past me." The black-coated croupiers began moving the mob from their tables, shoving them into a tight press, forcing them beneath the stairway toward the rear doors. Big, gangling Johnny Hanson was at the bar with Lon Carter, six-guns out, shoving the drinkers and barflies off the rail and into the larger group. And from outside, over all the noise and movement and voices inside the Palace, surged the hooting, yelling, cursing crowd of Kane's toughs.

Somebody's boots made a swift pound on the plank walk. A waddie appeared, running past the triple set of batwings, heading hell-for-leather eastward. Black-haired Georgie Nix leaped up past Pierce, his white teeth flashing in a fighting grin, the sawed-off shotgun tucked under one arm, a handful of cardboard cartridges in his hand. Then someone was standing beside Pierce, someone with a new gun that gleamed pathetically in his young brown fist. Jerry Albright.

"Damn you, kid!" yelled Pierce. "Get up to the

Joker's office. This place is going to be hotter than hell in a minute."

Lisa Albright must have seen her brother come from that back room leading off the balcony and go to the stairway, because Pierce saw her up there, struggling to get past Nix who had placed himself in the door of the office. Then Pierce couldn't wait to see if Nix held her, and he couldn't worry about Jerry any longer. Kane's crowd was surging through the doors!

They smashed through like a heavy roll of pounding surf. Big, heavy-bearded teamsters in muddy boots and dusty hickory jackets, waving huge old Sharps buffalo rifles. Two-bit gunnies, their Colts in white-knuckled hands, rushing through on high-heeled Justins. Drunken waddies, yelling and slapping their batwing chaps. All the swampers and bouncers and rotgut bartenders and cheap gamblers who hung around the west end. And right in the lead was dark-haired, beer-bellied Arvin Kane, shouting with the best of them, holding a six-gun in each hammy hand. Pierce had to admire him for that—whatever else he was, Kane was a fighter.

They must have seen each other about the same time. Pierce settled into a crouch, but this time it wasn't any slap-leather draw. Kane didn't slow down when he saw that lean, tall man on the stairs; he kept right on charging and his guns came up eagerly.

Pierce dropped his hammer and the Colt bucked in his hand. Kane didn't get one shot out. He stumbled and fell to his face on the floor, and his hoodlums trampled him under instantly. That shot seemed to set it off.

Before its sharp sound had died, the whole room was filled with rocking, deafening gun thunder. Standing there, driving slug after slug into the press, Pierce could see it all. He could see the mob spread out, overturning the roulette table and the faro table, tearing down the velvet hangings, shooting the chandeliers into shards of broken glass. He could see short, little Al McGowan on top of the green-topped monte table, the only one left standing. It was an island in a sea of men, and McGowan was holding it like a fort, a six-gun blazing in each hand.

From behind the long mahogany bar, the portly bartenders in their white aprons were slamming away with their own sixes. Tom Farril leaned over the balcony rail with his Winchester, levering and shooting, levering and shooting. On the other balcony, overlooking the hall from the right side, was another gunslick with a Winchester, creating awful carnage from that vantage point.

Man after man went down in that yelling, shooting mob. But the others surged over the bodies. A group charged the bar, crushing it back with their very weight, leaping across and clubbing at the barmen, smashing the huge gilt-framed mirror. Slugs chunked into the stairway around Pierce, chipping off wood, gouging holes in the red carpet, knocking a support from the railing. He reloaded, conscious that the kid was firing unsteadily from his side. Eldon Chiere stood at the head of the stairs, a little behind Pierce, and one of Kane's men dropped for every cold, methodical shot Chiere got out.

Inexorably the mob swept toward Pierce, across the smashed tables, over the dead and wounded, through the mess of glass that had spattered from the chandeliers. It was all a haze of gunfire and swimming smoke and howling men and acrid powder. Pierce shot a big teamster and the man went down under the boots of his fellows. He knocked a thin-faced gunman over backward with a slug through the chest. He shot a frock-coated gambler in the face. But they came on, a sweeping wave of them.

And suddenly Pierce was engulfed in that wave. They came charging up the stairs and his gun was empty. He reversed his gun and clubbed at them with the butt. Someone kicked him in the face and he jerked backward with the agony of pulped lips and broken teeth. A heavy boot landed in his midriff. A gun went off next to his ear, the slug tearing its burning path through his forearm. He felt Jerry Albright crushed up against him, felt him sagging under the pressure and blows of the maddened crowd. Pierce bent down to grab the boy, bent into that heat and stink of men, taking a knee in the groin.

Clubbing with his gun, kicking with his sharp heels, butting with his hatless head he fought back up the stairs, dragging the boy with him. He heard Chiere's methodical fire dimly, heard men scream around him, knew he was fighting free of them.

Then he was in the open, reloading. He took one dangerous glance over his shoulder. Farril and the gunmen from the other side of the balcony had joined Chiere. Pierce yelled hoarsely at them, then turned, swaying, thumbing his hammer. His gun bucked and rocked in his hand, thundering out shots. The toughs wavered halfway up the stairs. Then the three men behind Pierce were firing, moving down after the tall Texan, Winchesters and short guns bellowing.

Pierce leaped downward, bellowing at his men, telling them to drive Kane's dogs clear out into the street. Dimly he could see that McGowan was still up there on his table, down on one knee, but still shooting. And the men on the stairs in front of Pierce broke before Pierce's fire.

Farril stumbled and fell on his face, cursing bitterly. But Jerry Albright took Farril's place. He rose from where he had been crouching, wiping blood from his face, chunking new loads into that bright new gun, adding his shots to the din. The toughs from the west end were surging backward now, howling in defeat instead of battle lust and triumph. Pierce forced them across the litter of smashed tables and fallen hangings, taking a slug through his left shoulder and hardly feeling it.

A couple of croupiers joined him with their short belly guns. Hanson came from behind an overturned deal table he had been using for a barricade. A bloody bartender climbed over the smashed bar. McGowan leaped from his table, limping into the mess with his guns going.

The teamsters and swampers and drunken cowpunchers smashed their way out through the doors in a disorderly, panicky rout, taking the swinging batwings with them. Pierce was running forward, yelling crazily, shooting. His gun clicked on an empty chamber. And suddenly, from beneath an overturned table rose Kane's thick-shouldered bouncer, ugly face bloody and battered, a big Ward-Burton across his belly, dead bead on Pierce. Pierce was going forward too fast to stop himself. He threw his empty gun helplessly at the man, and saw it miss, spinning past the ugly head. And Pierce saw his death in that yawning gun muzzle. Then a body hurtled from somewhere to the side, blurred and big in Pierce's vision, a body that jerked to the thunder of that Ward-Burton. The slug went through that body, but it was deflected and slowed, and it only plucked at Pierce's shirt.

Then the body had sunk down in front of him. It was Jerry Albright. His new gun still smoked in his hand, and it was pointed at Kane's man, who was sinking to his knees, hands clutching his chest. Even as he had taken the Ward-Burton's bullet, the kid deftly nailed the bouncer.

Pierce kneeled, catching the boy in his arms, voice husky. "You damned fool kid. Why the hell didn't you go up to the Joker's office like I told you?"

The boy said weakly: "Now will you keep me on, Mister Pierce?"

Pierce had to blink his eyes, and he felt like a fool, and he was sick with self-disgust. "Sure, kid, we'll keep you on. You're a regular Billy the Kid."

If the boy had been going to live, Pierce wouldn't have encouraged him that way. But it was little enough to do for a kid whose life was leaking out of his belly so fast. His face didn't change expression when he realized the boy was dead. He laid him down gently and arose, the pain of his wounds not very sharp yet. The big room was strangely silent.

There were a few scattered shots down the street—Chiere and McGowan and one or two others finishing the job. The town was coming to life now that it was over. A shutter creaked, a door opened, and someone shouted, voice drifting dimly into the Palace.

And suddenly Lisa Albright was coming down the stairs, leather skirt swirling around her little half boots, face white. With a small moan she stumbled through the wreckage and fell to her knees beside Jerry, cradling his head in her arms. She didn't make any sound after that for a long time, just kneeled there, face white, eyes sightless with the sudden stunning grief.

Two men shoved through the smashed bat-wings. Big, square-shouldered Keeth Albright's iron-gray head was bare. Beside him Clem Albright looked very small. He walked slowly over to his son and daughter, looking down at the dead boy for a long time.

The Joker had picked his way through the mess, and Pierce could hear his heavy breathing. But for once the glib tongue was at a loss, the genial laugh was stilled. Pierce stared dully at the girl, feeling faint and dizzy now because of his wounds, head throbbing, arm beginning to seethe with pain.

Clem put his hand on Lisa's shoulder. "Come on, Daughter. Let's take the boy. We don't want to stay here any longer."

Lisa rose, turning slowly to face Pierce. Her voice was low and tense, filled with a bitter loathing. "I told you to leave him alone. And now you've murdered him. He was just a kid. He wasn't any gunman. I didn't realize I could ever hate anyone quite so much as I hate you, Emmet Pierce. You're the lowest, rottenest, dirtiest swine I know. . . ."

"Now, now, Daughter," said Clem quietly,

putting his arm around the girl. "It's all over. There's nothing we can do about it."

His glance met Pierce's for a moment, and the Texan saw a new light in the little, bald-headed man's quiet gray eyes. It seemed as if the death of his son had given him a new strength. Keeth bent over and picked up the boy as if he were a baby. He stood there with the body in his arms, facing Pierce, and the Joker. "By God," he said heavily. "You think you've got this town about taken over, Joker, but you'll learn different. I'll fight you with everything I've got, and I won't quit till you're dead, and this Poker Palace is razed to its last board."

He turned and stepped over the sprawled corpse of Arvin Kane, and walked outside. They could see his broad shoulders receding across the street, bent back a little to compensate for Jerry's weight. The Joker didn't say anything for a moment. Then he shrugged and, looking around the room, began to chuckle. "You did it, Emmet, m' boy. Nobody else could have stopped that mob, but you did. And now Kane's crowd is out. I can get the west end for a song. This little party doesn't mean a thing. We'll have the Palace running within the week, twice as big, twice as loud. I'll knock out the east wall and extend the lower floor fifty feet on out. I'll get chandeliers three times as big as the ones they shot down . . . I'll get dancing girls from Saint Louis, and turn those rooms upstairs into private gambling salons. I tell you, Emmet . . ."

He went on talking, that smile growing. But Pierce swayed a little on his spraddled legs, hardly hearing. He looked about him at the terrific carnage. Arvin Kane lay with his legs beneath an overturned table, hands still gripping those six-guns. The bouncer huddled almost at Pierce's feet, Jerry Albright's lead in his dead chest. The velvet and silken hangings had been pulled down over the smashed tables, and here and there they bulged a little, covering a body. The broken glass from the chandeliers lay spattered over everything, glinting fitfully in the light from the lamps. And from the smashed batwing doors to the stairway lay the dead and wounded—Kane's two-bit gun-men and tinhorn gamblers, the Joker's triggermen and bartenders, some piled up where a volley had swept them, others lying in ones or twos, blood showing red against faces or chests or bellies. A man on the far side of the room groaned.

Pierce spat out some teeth and some blood, and his laugh was a little hysterical. "She was right, Joker. She said I was the lowest, rottenest, dirtiest swine she knew, and she was right. I was getting some crazy idea that I was too good for your dirty deals, wasn't I? But I should have known better. You and me, we're two of a kind, Joker. We belong together, right down here in the gutter with the killers like Chiere and Nix, and the toughs like Kane and his mob. I couldn't climb out of it if I wanted to. I was born in it, and I'll die in it."

V

Pierce sat idly at one of the back tables of the new Poker Palace, with its huge chandeliers, its added room on the east side, its dancing girls. An attendant passed him, turning up the oil lamps that lined the walls. The piano tinkled from up front, flanked by potted plants.

It had been several weeks since the battle. The Joker had Benton sewed up tight now. Already he had bought out Kane's holdings in the west end, tearing down the cheap saloons and the bawdy houses. In their places he was erecting a three-story frame hotel that would rival the Douglas House in Omaha for size and sumptuousness, and a huge livery stable that would stretch half a block with its half a hundred stalls.

Charlie Torrance had proved his look of being the kind to drift whichever way the wind blew. The Joker had promised his support in the coming election, and Torrance was now as much his man as Chiere or Nix. He told the council the Joker refused to pay the tax, and the council was helpless, seeing that Torrance was their duly appointed representative of the law.

True to his word, the Joker had turned the rooms leading off the balcony into private gambling salons. There were more than a few local politicians who had a predilection for gambling, but who didn't want to be seen doing it in public. A back stairway to the second floor of the Palace lured many of them to those salons, and sooner or later they found themselves compromised.

Georgie Nix came down the stairs, moving through the crowd to Pierce. He looked at the man lighting the lamps, shook his head. "I don't like the way those lamps set. It was a wonder they didn't start a fire when Kane and his crowd shot 'em down. Only take a little to catch the hangings." He turned that white-toothed smile on Pierce, and there seemed to be something behind it, a speculation. "By the way, the Joker wants you up in his office."

Pierce went reluctantly up the stairs, past the hard-eyed gunslick by the office door. The Joker was leaning back in his chair, and he had changed immensely since they first hit Benton. Greed had turned the twinkle in his eyes to an avaricious glitter. His paunch was approaching the prodigious, and he rarely left the room now.

"Hello, Emmet, m' boy," he said. "We've been discussing Dillon. Decided he's getting dangerous. Drunk most of the time now, shoots off his mouth too much. His third of the profits are just wasted on him. He's too swathed to do more than throw the money away on liquor and the monte table."

Pierce looked around the room. Chiere stood beside the desk, sallow face a mask from which his dead eyes regarded Pierce with cold indifference. Al McGowan sat on the arm of a chair, picking his teeth, grinning.

"If you've talked it over with the boys," said Pierce, "why bring me in?"

The Joker said dryly: "Remember what I used to say, Emmet, about my talents and your gun? Well, it's been mostly my talents these last weeks. We don't want you to get rusty. And, after all, wasn't it Dillon who tried to have you and me dusted off in this very room?"

"You're not going to get rid of him that way," said Pierce. "Not that poor, drunk, helpless fool."

"Why the sudden distaste for killing, Emmet?" said the Joker. "You used to do it so easily."

"I've never murdered a man in cold blood," said Pierce intensely. "I'm not starting now. . . ." He stopped to the sound of heavy, unsteady footsteps coming down the balcony and through the door behind him. Dillon lurched by Pierce, eyes bleary, cold cigar drooping from one side of a slack mouth. Bat followed him in, head gleaming, .45s in his broad, black belt.

"You wanna see me, Joker?" asked Dillon thickly.

The Joker turned to Al McGowan. "Close the door, Al." Then he looked at Dillon, and his grin utterly lacked any mirth; it was cold and deadly. "Yes, partner, I wanted to see you."

His eyes went past Dillon to Pierce. There seemed to be a question in them as he spoke Pierce's name, as if he were giving Pierce another, last chance.

"Emmet?"

Pierce remained silent, stubborn refusal in his long face. A sudden flush crept into the Joker's unhealthy-looking cheeks, and that little vein began pulsing in his forehead. When he said Chiere's name, there was no question.

"Chiere."

The gunman's wasp-waisted body didn't move. Only his hands, dipping down, up. His first thundering shot caught Dillon dead center, slamming him backward into Bat. The bullet-headed man caught his boss with one arm, stumbling with the weight, clawing at a .45 with his free hand. Chiere's other Paterson roared. Bat made a heavy sound, falling. Dillon collapsed on top of him.

Pierce hadn't moved. He looked down at them for a long moment, lips white, eyes sated. His voice was a flat monotone when he finally spoke. "Joker, that was the most unnecessary thing you ever did. I guess I haven't really known you up until right now." Then he turned on his heel, opening the heavy door, moving out into the brightly lit balcony. And a sick disgust swept through him.

• • •

A hot wind struck at Pierce as he cantered from between the double row of buildings at the west end of town, and into the open, wheel-rutted road. There was a surprising grace to his long, awkward-looking body as he sat his Brazos saddle, at ease for the first time in many weeks. Beside him rode Eldon Chiere on a small gray, left hand gloved, right hand bare, hanging habitually just above his gun. Behind them creaked the big Studebaker wagons, loaded with bales of barb wire.

Only one man had stood before the Joker's rise in Benton—Keeth Albright. The gambler had tried desperately to get control of him, or break him. He had withheld loans and deposits from his brother's bank until Clem had been forced to close his doors and take his daughter out to Keeth's spread, ruined, disgraced. Though Keeth lost some money when Clem's bank folded, he still had his tight little Bar-Over-Nine outfit with its small but tough crew of cowpunchers—and he still remained a thorn in the Joker's side. The Joker's mind, however, was a ceaseless process of devious, crooked machinations. Even as hewas trying to get control of Keeth Albright in one way, he was devising a dozen others in case he failed.

The country around Benton had always been free and open range, and the Bitter Creek region had been a communal watering place for all the cattlemen. For most of its course, Bitter Creek was a roaring mountain river, passing through wild gorges, completely inaccessible to cattle. But just below Devil's Head Peak, it quieted down, running through a peaceful valley, banks broad and sandy, forming an easy approach to the water. During the summer, when the other holes and rivulets dried up, this section of Bitter Creek was the only watering place in the district. Under the new Homestead Act, the Joker saw his opportunity. He had his triggermen file claim on sections of land adjacent to that quiet, accessible portion of Bitter Creek, until their holdings formed a strip between Devil's Head Park to the north and Pumpkin Bluffs to the south. Pierce was riding to put up a fence on that strip, a fence that would cut off the approach of cattle from either side.

Ever since the Joker had gotten rid of Dillon, Pierce had told himself he was pulling up stakes. He realized his life wasn't worth a plugged *peso* now. The Joker had known how things stood when Pierce refused to shoot Dillon—perhaps it had been as good a way as any of finding out. But though he knew he should leave, something held Pierce. This bizarre crazy structure they had built up was as much his as it was the Joker's. He had built up the army of triggermen, had picked them with such care. He had watched the thing grow from a money belt full of gold pieces they had fleeced from the suckers on the trail north, to a giant organization that engulfed Benton and the country around it, controlling the lives of almost every one within its reach. He hadn't cared much about it at first—he had just ridden along with it. But now it was a part of him. The fabric of his life was woven into it. Wanting to leave, wanting to saddle his roan and hit the trail, he knew he couldn't. He would have to ride the thing out because he was a part of it.

They turned north off the road, moving slowly through a broken bit of badlands, purple and yellow buttes, a few stunted cottonwoods. To their left and slightly ahead loomed the towering Devil's Head Peak, lodgepole and white pine climbing its rugged slopes. The wagons made heavy going of it over the rough ground. Several times the riders had to tie dally ropes onto axles or hounds and help pull.

Tom Farril waited for them on the rise ahead. He had taken a couple of slugs through the ribs in the battle with Kane, and the bandaging beneath his patched flannel shirt made his body look thicker. He eased himself forward on his raw-boned jughead and called to Pierce.

"Thought you'd never git here. Been some of Albright's waddies snoopin' around. I think they know what we're up to."

"Where do we start stringing the fence?" Pierce asked.

Farril pointed to the high Pumpkin Bluffs

beyond a motte of scraggly alamos. "From them on down this here rise and up the Devil's Head slope. It'll close off the water completely."

Pierce turned in his saddle, directing Nix to take the Studebakers over to the bluffs. When he had finished, Chiere asked: "Hadn't we better take a look at those Bar-Over-Nine men?"

"Where'd you spot 'em?" Pierce asked Farril.

"Up on the mountain, nosin' around the fringe of timber," said the sloe-eyed Oklahoman. "We could git up behind 'em by ridin' down to the crick and workin' up the slope on their right."

Pierce nodded and urged his horse into a trot toward the river. He could hear Chiere and Farril following. They ground-hitched their mounts in some hip-high bluestem in the bottoms, and worked up the slope, through the tall stands of lodgepole. Finally, they neared a boulder-strewn clearing. Farril stooped and scuttled to a big out-cropping rock. Pierce followed, stretching out on the boulder, warm from the sun. The Oklahoman pointed down the slope.

"Down there," he said. "Where that bunch of scrub oak is."

Pierce craned over the lip of the rock. Before him lay the sweep of hillside, stretching down for half a mile, clear of trees. Near the bottom grew some stunted, twisted oaks, beyond them a fringe of tall pine. There were no Bar-Over-Nine cowpunchers visible.

Pierce heard the soft, sly scrape of leather chaps against the boulder, and from the corner of his eye saw Farril drawing away from him, rising. With a sudden understanding, Pierce rolled violently over on his back, grabbing awkwardly at his .45. There was no malice or personal hatred in Chiere's cold, dead eyes, only a certain deliberate purpose. His gun was already coming up, a gleaming blur.

The flame and the thunder and the sudden jarring pain of the heavy bullet through his chest were all one to Pierce. And even as he was slammed back against the rock, his thumb was dropping the hammer of his own gun, and that gun was bucking its one time in his hand. Dimly he saw Chiere go down, crumpling up like a rag doll with all the sawdust leaking out of it. Then a roaring wave of agony swept Pierce down into a blackness without bottom. The last thing he felt was the boulder against his back.

The hard warmth of the rock had changed to a softness beneath him, and when he opened his eyes, it wasn't Chiere standing there. It was Lisa Albright. She had her dark hair done up with a bright ribbon and a white, doeskin vest over her flannel shirt. There was pity in her eyes, no hate. He tried to rise.

She kneeled beside him, forcing him back. "You're not going to get up for a long time. Chiere just about finished you. Our waddies heard the shot and trailed up the slope. Chiere was dead."

He could feel a dull throbbing pain in the middle of his chest that grew sharper as he regained full consciousness. He was lying in a big four-poster bed. There were several solid white pine chairs in the room, a china pitcher on the table beside him, chintz curtains in the windows. He thought the Bar-Over-Nine house was nice.

"Why . . . why did you even bother with me, after all that's happened, after what I did?" he asked.

"If a man needs help as badly as you did, it doesn't matter who he is or what he did," she said. "Weren't you ever taught that?"

"I wasn't ever taught anything," he muttered. "I had to learn all by myself."

"That's probably your trouble." She smiled faintly. "I'm going to get you some hot soup now, and I don't want you moving about. Understand?"

The girl was right about his not getting up for a long time. He lay there in that pleasant room for weeks, while the summer passed and fall set in. For a while, there was a stiffness between him and Lisa.

But sometimes in the evening she would come in to build a fire in the big grout fireplace, and sit a while with the firelight catching a shine in her dark eyes, glinting in her hair. He found himself telling her of his boyhood down near the border, his wild, harsh boyhood, fighting men before he was twelve, learning how to shoot a gun too soon and too well.

"I wondered how you'd ever fallen in with men like the Joker. You don't seem their kind, somehow. Oh, I know you're a gunman, a killer, but there's something square in you, too, Pierce. I realize now it wasn't your fault Jerry got killed. He told me several times that you wouldn't hire him."

"The Joker and Nix and Chiere were the only kind of men I knew, really," he said. "I didn't know there was a man big enough to take his enemy in and keep him from dying."

"It's difficult to think of you as an enemy any more." She smiled. "You can't help finding out a lot about a person when you live in the same house with them. Keeth might hate you because you were with the Joker, but he admires you as a man. He said it would take a man with your strength to smash the Joker's hold on Benton. He said he wished you were on our side."

Being with her like that, talking with her stirred things inside him, things no other woman had ever stirred. He knew now why he had tried to justify himself to her when they first met, knew that first restlessness had been because of her. He wanted to tell her what was going on in him, but he couldn't. He was Emmet Pierce, a gunman, a killer.

Finally, he was able to get out of bed, able to sit at the supper table in the dining room. Clem's wife had died, but Keeth's housekeeper, Mrs. Weatherby, made up for it. She was a big, homey woman, not very pretty but jolly and good-natured, mothering Clem and Lisa as if they were her own, and accepting Pierce openly, without reservation.

Clem was the friendliest. He played checkers with Pierce by the big fireplace. The Texan would watch the little man when he was bent over a move, baldhead gleaming, eyes mild and kind behind his spectacles. And Pierce realized he had never known up until now what friendship really was.

The fight between the Joker and Albright had come out in the open now. Time and time again, Keeth tried to break through the gun guards on the fence, and get his cattle to the river. But his handful of waddies were helpless against the professional gunmen riding that barb wire. His cattle were dying swiftly. Gradually he lost his crew. He had sent three of them down to Laramie with the Joker's lead in their guts, not trusting the doctor at Benton. Another cowpuncher was dead out in that little hollow between Devil's Head and Pumpkin Bluffs.

Keeth became so short-handed that Clem took to riding out with him. It was a futile, stubborn gesture. And one night, the gray-haired Bar-Over-

Nine corporal brought his brother back over his saddle.

Pierce and Lisa were sitting in the big parlor with its barn-sash windows drawn tight against the early winter chill, the firelight flickering across the rough, hand-hewn beams. Perhaps Lisa sensed how Pierce felt about her, for an awkward silence had grown between them. The girl rose as hoofs pounded in through the split-rail fence outside, halting in front of the door.

"I hope Uncle Keeth hasn't lost any more of the boys," she said. "They've been so loyal through all this."

When she opened the big door, he could see the line of hipshot ponies standing in a bunch by the front porch. The half dozen remaining waddies were gathered around one horse, lifting some-one off. Lisa's voice was sharp, terrified.

"Dad, Dad . . ."

The tall, taciturn foreman named Landers and Keeth Albright carried the pitiful body of Clem Albright into his bedroom and laid him out on the four-poster bed, leaving Lisa alone with him. Standing in the parlor, they could hear her hopeless sobbing. Then even that sound stopped, and for a long moment, it was painfully silent. Keeth's face seemed ten years older, grief and impotent anger deepening the lines about his strong mouth, narrowing his steely eyes to mere slits. He had tried so hard to be just and tolerant toward Pierce, but his brother's death let down the flood gates of the terrible emotions he had held inside himself ever since Jerry had died. He turned on the Texan, eyes blazing behind their narrowed lids, mouth twisting in his rage.

"You did this, Pierce. Clem was killed by Nix . . . your man. You're to blame just as much as the Joker for all the hell we're going through, for all the pain and misery and death that's swept Benton. I wish to hell I'd left you there on the Devil's Head. I wish I had the guts to fill your belly just as full as Clem's is. . . ." He broke off, drawing a deep, shuddering breath.

Lisa's voice turned them all. She stood in the doorway of her dad's bedroom, dry-eyed, something infinitely proud in the line of her straight young body. "You're wrong, Uncle Keeth. We're as much to blame as Pierce. We could have stopped this at the start. If Dad had refused to give those mortgages to the Joker, if he'd been strong enough to see his bank fail then, we would have stood a chance. And if you and Rickett and Wells had gotten together at first, you would have had the strength to fight back. Now it's too late. You'll never get anywhere butting your head against that barb-wire fence. There's only one way to finish it now."

Pierce remembered Clem as he'd sat there, playing checkers, the mild, kind eyes, the friendship he'd had for the man he should have hated.

The Joker had killed him. And Keeth Albright, and Mrs. Weatherby, standing there pale and helpless in the kitchen door, and Lisa, who was meant for life instead of death. Sooner or later they would go down under the Joker's heel; they would die like Kane, and Clem, and Jerry. Pierce felt a sudden growing bitter hatred for the fat, chuckling gambler. And he knew what he had to do.

"She's right, Albright," he said. "There's only one way left to stop this thing, to smash it."

Keeth looked at him in bitter disgust. "Kane and his whole mob tried that way. They couldn't do it. What chance would we have? The thing sounds almost funny coming from you, the Joker's number one man."

"I told Lisa a long time ago I wasn't anybody's man," said Pierce. "Do you think I'd still be in with that fat rat when he tried to have me killed? You saved my life, Albright, you took me in when you should have left me to die. Your brother befriended me when he should have hated me. Let me help you now. Let me ride with you into Benton. You said I helped build this crazy thing. It's my right to smash it."

Keeth turned to the fireplace, spreading his strong hands out on the mantel, face twisted with mingled emotions. Finally he turned back. "As much as I've always hated you and what you stood for, Pierce, I've admired you as a man. You have strength, and you don't break your word. Give me that word now, and we'll ride to Benton."

"You have my word," said Pierce, grinning. "I'll ride beside you to hell, Albright, if you'll let me."

VI

A snow had begun to fall when they reached the outskirts of Benton. It cast a white, fresh mantle over the town, covering the roofs lightly, making little drifts up against the plank sidewalk on either side. Pierce wore his old Stetson, and one of Keeth's Mackinaws over his vest, gun buckled around on the outside.

Lisa had insisted on coming with them. She drove the buckboard behind the little cavalcade, muffled to her chin in a thick buffalo coat. A small, growing excitement swept Pierce as he dismounted outside the last building at the west end of Main. They would all be there, the men he had chosen so carefully, a veritable army of men standing between him and the Joker. He was glad, for a moment, that Chiere was out of it.

Yet, for all his utterly cold, inhuman skill, Eldon Chiere had never been the most dangerous. Tom Farril, for instance. His savage eagerness to use his gun put edge on his draw that made him much more of a threat than the sallow-faced, impersonal Chiere. And Georgie Nix was even deadlier. Nix had a flash and a rare, brilliant style that neither Farril nor Chiere could match. There was one man, however, who topped Nix. Little stubby lethal Al McGowan. There was something infinitely terrible about his bulldog stubbornness that no flash or style could equal. And the Joker, of course, master of them all—the incomparable, sly, disarming Joker who had more menace in his little finger than his whole crew of triggermen had in all their guns. Bucking a regular slap-leather draw was child's play compared to facing the Joker's confusing prestidigitations, not knowing where a gun was coming from, or when it was coming, or even how many guns there would be.

Pierce turned to Albright, who stood in front of the foreman and the waddies. "It'd be suicide to try and take the Palace the way Kane did. You put Landers and a couple of waddies in that store by the bank across from the Palace. They can keep anyone from coming out. The back stairs to the Palace's second story lead up from the inside of the jail. You can take the rest of your hands up that way. Watch out for the guards."

"And you?" asked Albright.

Pierce grinned faintly. "From that boarding house next to the jail, a man can reach the jail roof. And from the jail roof, he can jump to the overhang above the Palace's front doors. The window of the Joker's office looks out on that overhang. I think that's my job, don't you?"

Albright nodded, turned to Lisa. "You stay here till it's over . . . one way or the other."

Lisa was looking at Pierce. Her eyes were wide, and there was something in them that made him wish he had told her what was inside him. Now it was too late. If he got out alive, maybe.

He turned and began walking east. Behind him, the girl's voice was sharp, fearful. "Pierce. . . ."

He kept on walking, not turning back, and Albright followed with the cowpunchers. Some of the gunnies didn't sleep at the Poker Palace. As Pierce passed the Joker's new white frame hotel with its green shutters and sedate front yard, a tall, lanky figure in barrel-leg chaps and patched flannel shirt came out the door. Tom Farril and Emmet Pierce saw each other about the same time. Farril stopped with one high-heeled boot on the porch's bottom step, the other on the sidewalk. His voice sounded loud.

"Emmet Pierce. My God, I thought you was dead."

Pierce was rusty from the long weeks of confinement. If Farril had triggered from where he stood, he might have stayed alive. But it was a long shot between them, and his very eagerness to kill was his undoing. In that instant after he spoke, surprise melted from his sloe-eyes—he lurched forward into a run, his draw a blurred dip of the hand. Farril's gun cleared leather before

Pierce's. But the jar of his boots on the hard walk threw him off, and his first shot whined past Pierce. Then the Texan's gun bellowed once from just above the edge of his holster. Farril's second slug pounded into the walk before him as he went down on his face into the soft snow.

Pierce stood looking at him for an instant, thinking, this is the first one, then, and there are so many better ones between me and the Joker. Then he turned and broke into a run because he knew it had to be fast now. The shots had drawn attention. A man came from the barbershop, lather still on his chin. He looked for a long moment at that tall, long-legged figure pounding down the sidewalk toward him. Then he lurched across the wheel-rutted street toward the Palace, bits of lather dropping off his face, shouting: "It's Pierce. Emmet Pierce! He's come back, dammit, he's come back!"

The name seemed to have a magic effect. A pair of gunslicks popped through the batwings of the Palace. Another legged it from the general store, a sixteen-shot Henry in his hand. Someone shoved open a window of the office above the barbershop and began shooting.

Keeth Albright's gun bellowed from behind Pierce. One of the gunnies who had burst from the Palace pitched onto the sidewalk. Two Bar-Over-Nine cowpunchers cut across the street behind Landers, Winchesters bobbing at their hips. The man with the Henry tried to duck back in his door. But one of those Winchesters barked, and he sat down against the baseboards of the building, head sinking onto his chest. Slugs chipping wood at his feet, Pierce threw himself into the boarding house, shouting at Albright: "Good luck, Albright."

Then he was running down the hall, taking the rickety stairway in long leaps. The smell of cooking hung in the hall above. He turned toward the window that overlooked the street. A man lurched out of a doorway. He saw Pierce and backed against the wall, hands jerking upward.

"Okay, Pierce, I ain't slapping leather."

Pierce passed him, raising the window to throw a leg over the sill and drop to the shingled overhang. From there, he half slid, half crawled to the sloping hip roof of the jail. He could see the whole street spread out below. Landers and his two men had flopped down in the doorway of the store, and their Winchesters kept the Joker's triggermen helplessly inside the Palace. The two gunmen who had first come through the gambling hall's batwings lay on the plank walk. And down at the west end, Pierce could see Farril's body, and beyond that, Lisa and the buckboard and the horses.

Then he was sliding down the other side of the hip roof, coming up hard against the straight wall of the Palace's second story. He worked forward, taking a breath before he made the long drop to the Palace's overhang in front.

The man above the barbershop began potting at Pierce. Pierce turned on his back and sent two slugs through the window, shattering glass. The man ducked back and quit potting. Cuffing off his big Stetson so it wouldn't show, Pierce rose to his knees and peered through the window of the Joker's office. The big brass-studded door was ajar, and the room was empty. Pierce tried to raise the lower section of the window with one hand. It stuck, and he holstered his gun to heave with both hands. The window gave, rose with a shriek. He sat on the sill, drawing his legs up and over and onto the floor.

Georgie Nix must have heard the window. He stepped into the room from the balcony before Pierce had a chance to rise from his sitting position on the sill. And Pierce didn't try to rise then. He sat there with his hand hovering just above his gun, waiting for Nix to make his play. But Georgie Nix had a vanity that matched his flash and color, the incredible vanity of a pro gunman. He showed his white teeth in that grin.

"Well, Emmet Pierce. The man who smoked down Chiere. But then he never was too fast, was he? I don't think you've ever met a really fast man, Pierce."

"Like you?" asked the Texan.

Nix's smile grew. "Yeah, like me. Y'know, ever

87

since I knew you down on the border, I've wondered if maybe they didn't overrate you. Stand up, Pierce, and let's find out now. You and me, even-steven. Go ahead, stand up."

Pierce rose slowly, speculation in his narrowed eyes. Those long weeks in bed hadn't done his draw any good. He couldn't forget how slow he'd been with Farril. It couldn't be that slow now, not against the blinding speed of big, black-haired Georgie Nix.

That swaggering ego was in Nix's confident voice. "I'll even give you an edge, Pierce. You make the first play. What more could you ask?"

Pierce set himself. No rustiness this time, no slowed reflexes. If that clash with Farril hadn't taken the kinks out, but habit and instinct were skill, not thought. He let his words empty his mind.

"All right, Nix. . . ."

Nix's white teeth still showed in his daredevil grin. He slapped leather so soon after Pierce that their draws seemed simultaneous. Yet Pierce's gun bellowed before Nix's quite left leather. Nix took a step backward with the slug through his chest. His gun slid back into its holster from a relaxing hand. His smile had turned to a look of amazement, as if, even in death, he couldn't believe Pierce was the faster man.

Pierce punched out his four empties, shoved in fresh rimfires. Al McGowan would be out there, more dangerous than either Nix or Farril. Pierce had faced most types of gunmen, and the kind he had come to recognize as the deadliest were the stubborn, blind, obstinate fools who just didn't know when to quit. And that was Al McGowan.

Nerves tightening, Pierce stepped around Nix and into the doorway. And he saw why the office had been empty. The Poker Palace was on fire!

It seemed a long time ago that Nix had expressed concern over those oil lamps socketed so near the hangings. Landers and his two waddies were still shooting from across the street, keeping the space around the batwings cleared. One of their slugs must have knocked a lamp down, and it had set fire to the velvet drapes, the silken tapestries. The crowd in the lower hall was milling around crazily. Some of them were trying to push out the rear way, others swarmed around at the foot of the stairway. The flickering crackle of fire formed a menacing undertone to the terrified yelling of the men, the few frightened screams of women.

McGowan and the Joker stood at the head of the stairs. Apparently they had meant to escape to the first floor, but a huge, blazing beam had fallen across the stairway, barring that escape, crushing some of the crowd below. The Joker was a mountainous figure there in the crazy light of the flames, his expensive frock coat and flowered waistcoat covering a monumental paunch, his bejowled face gleaming with sweat. He saw Pierce, and his mouth opened for a moment in surprise. Then he began backing on down the balcony, putting McGowan in between Pierce and himself.

McGowan stepped away from the railing, drawing his twin .44s, spreading his legs in that stubborn way. Here was no Farril with his eagerness, no Nix with his flash. Here was an infinitely more lethal man, the man who had refused to retreat from that green-topped roulette table in the face of all Arvin Kane's shooting, howling mob from the west end. Yet, what was it the Joker had said about Pierce? "Good old single-track Pierce. Get you set on a road and all hell and high water can't get you off till you reach the end." Pierce was on that road now. They made a pair, little bulldog Al McGowan and long-legged, awkward-looking, single-minded Emmet Pierce.

It was a long way from the doorway of the Joker's office down the balcony and around to the head of the stairs. And it was typical of McGowan that he held his fire. Pierce moved forward, gaining speed, breaking into a run. Farril's aim had been thrown off by the hard pound of his high heels, and Pierce knew he was taking the same chance. But he wasn't fool enough to advance on McGowan walking.

Still, the short little gunman held his fire, serene, unruffled, terrible in his grim patience. Pierce was halfway to the turn when he threw down, the first to shoot, gun loud above the crackle of flame. The bullet hit McGowan. He swayed forward and had to drop one of his guns so he could catch the balcony rail. Holding himself up like that, he opened fire.

Pierce's running, bobbing figure made a poor target for the wounded man, shooting in the flickering red deceptive light of the flames. A slug smashed wood behind the Texan. Another ricocheted off the molding. Still charging like a loco Brahma, Pierce dropped his hammer on another chamber, another. One of those slugs found their mark, too. McGowan slid farther down the railing. But he cocked his gun for another shot.

The crazy, exhilarating, blood-red excitement of battle was roaring through Pierce now, and nothing short of death could have stopped him. He careened around the turn in the balcony, throwing down for a fourth time. But one of McGowan's bullets slammed through his side.

Pierce lurched, stumbled, unable to get his shot out. He didn't fall though. Momentum carrying him forward, he lined up on McGowan again, thumbing at his hammer desperately. The stubborn little triggerman took that one, too, and tried to keep on fighting. But his grip on the rail slipped. His gun barrel wavered down. The last shot he got out as he sank to the floor, hit wood at Pierce's feet.

Pierce went to his knees, then, putting out a hand to keep himself from going farther. Shakily he rose, looking for the Joker.

The balcony ran clear across the rear and up either side of the Palace, forming a big U, with the Joker's office at one end, a bunk room for the gunmen at the other. The Joker had reached that bunk room, was fumbling with the door. Pierce began to move forward again.

It was the kingpin of them all now, the man who had more menace in his little finger than the army of triggermen had in all their guns. Pierce made the turn in the balcony, blood seeping through the fingers he clutched over his wound. His face was burned, blackened, eyebrows singed. He didn't know how many beans he had left in his wheel, one, maybe two. There was no time to reload. The Joker himself had said he'd seen this coming, this clash between Pierce and him. He was the man to be prepared, with his million tricks and his magic hands; he would leave nothing to chance.

For a moment, the smoke swept away. Pierce caught sight of the gross gambler there at the end of the balcony. The door to the bunk room must have been locked, for the Joker had turned around. He saw Pierce and he held out his hands, empty.

"I'm not heeled, Emmet. You aren't the kind of man to shoot me in cold blood. You said that yourself."

A blazing timber fell in front of Pierce, shooting flames hiding the Joker again. All down that paunchy rat's back trail was the numberless army of men who had tried to buck the cold murder beneath his disarming smile, and always the Joker came out ace high, still smiling. Now Pierce was bucking it, pitting his one skill against the myriad talents in that murderous knave's pale fingers.

The Joker called through the smoke. "Let's start all over again, Emmet, m' boy, let's hit the trail again. There are other towns, other suckers."

"It won't work, Joker," choked the Texan. "You can't lie like you used to. I know you're heeled. Go ahead, do your tricks, Joker, play your cards."

The Joker must have realized, then, that only one thing would stop Emmet Pierce. As Pierce stepped across that burning rafter, bursting from the black, swirling smoke into the open, the Joker's hands were still empty. Pierce knew it was coming, had been expecting it, yet he was taken a little off guard when a Derringer appeared suddenly in one of those empty hands, when a sawed-off belly gun slid from nowhere into the other.

Coughing, eyes stinging and half blinded,

surprise taking the edge from his reflexes, Pierce squeezed his trigger. Even as he did, that Derringer was blasting. The soft-nosed slug struck Pierce's gun hand. His Colt jarred upward uncontrollably in smashed fingers, and he knew he missed. A terrible triumph twisted the Joker's face as his belly-gun roared. Few men would have tried the border shift then, even fewer would have succeeded. But as that belly-gun's slug smashed through Pierce's shoulder, as he was falling forward with agony searing his whole conscious-ness, he jerked his right arm and flipped the Colt from his mutilated right hand into his good left one. The Joker saw it. His smoking Derringer steadied in a white-knuckled hand.

But the bloody handle of Pierce's Colt was already slapping into his left palm. His thumb was working the hammer. The Joker never fired that .51 slug from his Derringer's other barrel, because Pierce's gun bellowed, and the two men weren't ten feet apart—and an *hombre* who had been a triggerman most of his life couldn't miss at that distance, even if he was filled with lead and falling on his face.

The Joker grunted sickly, tottered sideways. And before Pierce hit the floor, he had that one last look at the Joker, a look that would be burned into his memory forever. All the greed and lust for power that had lain dormant in the

Joker till he took over Benton showed in his face now. His mouth, once so capable of such a charming disarming grin, was shrunken and twisted with avarice. His little eyes had lost their twinkle and they glittered like a snake's eyes from deep within the revolting puffiness of his fat, swollen cheeks. Overriding the avarice and greed and lust was a fear, stamped into his features by death.

Then he was crashing over against the balcony railing, his great weight smashing it beneath him. Above the cries and the shouts and the roar of the flames, the heavy thud of this body hitting the floor below held a sickening finality.

Pierce tried to rise, but somehow all the will to live had been squeezed out of him in those last few intense moments. An army of greedy red flames raced toward him and he heard the groan of collapsing beams overhead. His head sank into his arms and he resigned himself to death. Then hands were tugging at him. A tall gray-haired man and a waddy, their faces grimy with soot and powder smoke, were lifting him, carrying him back along the balcony. Albright had made it up the back stairs by then.

They took him through one of the small, private salons. A table was overturned, cards and chips spilled across the floor in a colorful pool. Two men lay in the door of the rear stairway, a Bar-Over-Nine cowpuncher and one of the Joker's gunnies. Farther down was another triggerman, and at the bottom lay Johnny Hanson, grotesque in death. Charlie Torrance had never been a brave man. He must have sloped out when the shooting started, for his front office was empty.

They sat Pierce down on the edge of the sidewalk across the street. Someone was beside him, soft hands supporting him. And he thought it was funny how a girl could make you feel so much better like that by just touching you. The sawbones and the barber began cutting his shirt away.

"Will he, will he . . . ?" began Lisa.

The doctor grumped: "You should have called me about that wound in his chest. But if he lived with that, I guess these little nicks won't do any harm."

"With his million tricks, the Joker couldn't buck your one, Pierce, and I guess he knew it all along." Albright grinned. "And now he's dead, his whole rotten organization wiped out. You did it, Pierce, you kept your word."

"You got started on the wrong trail down there in Río Hondo, Emmet," murmured Lisa. "But you can forget that trail. You can start a new one here in Benton, start it with a clean slate."

Pierce spoke weakly. "I wanted to ask you this a long time ago, Lisa, but I didn't think I had the right. If you really mean that about the new trail, I'd like you to ride it with me."

She smiled softly. "Clear up to the end, Emmet Pierce."

They turned, then, to the blazing Palace. The townsmen had formed a bucket brigade, but all they could do was keep the other buildings wet so the fire wouldn't spread. The Poker Palace was a total loss. Somehow, the leaping flames were symbolic, wiping out all the pain and greed and death that had swept Benton, purging Pierce's dark past and leaving the future bright and clean and new.

WHERE
HELL'S COYOTES
HOWL

I

The firelight caught the strange, puckered scar pattern high on one side of his face as Laramie Drake paced restlessly back and forth in front of the fireplace. He had taken off his coat, but the strap harnessing his Knuckle Duster beneath one armpit still gleamed across the white shirt drawn taut over the heft of his shoulder. There was something sardonic about the twist of his thin, mobile lips, and his black eyes roved the room almost angrily.

"Listen." Etienne Villeneu, sitting gross and cheerful in the big Spanish armchair they had brought from the Coronado house, had begun whetting his pair of carving knives again. "Listen, Drake, you didn't think you could throw off the old life with one shrug of your shoulders, did you? You want to retire at thirty-five? *Voila!* Retire. But you've been a gambler most of your life, and you got to give yourself time to get accustomed to this. Now let me tell you about the *Filets de Levraut a la Mornay* I am planning for supper. You trim off the filets of two leverets . . . *compre?* . . . two young hares . . ."

"All right, all right." Laramie Drake waved a long-fingered hand, supple and pale from so many years with the cards. "So we're having

Filets of Rabbit Mornay. That's fine. I know exactly how you prepare it. After ten years with you, I could write a recipe book."

"Hare, not rabbit. You never let me finish telling you how to cook *Filets de Levraut*, Drake," pouted Etienne. He weighed nearly two hundred and fifty pounds and stood many inches shorter than Drake's five-ten, and his white apron rose in a series of jolly bulges from fat thighs to triple chins, a waxed mustache looking as if it held up the red bulb of his nose. He must have realized how Drake had stopped pacing, for he looked up from his carving knives. "Eh?"

Drake ran one hand through his thick black hair, heavy brows drawing down over his eyes as he tried to hear it again. "Sounded like someone riding their horse pretty hard."

Etienne spat upon the whetstone. "You are just jumpy. Who would be coming this far into the Tanques Verdes at night? When you picked a spot for your chateau, you really wanted to get away from Tucson."

"No, listen." Drake's shoes made a soft thud across the red and black Navajo rug to the heavy oak door, and he swung it open. Then the tattoo of a running horse came clearly, and Etienne hoisted himself out of the armchair, his white chef's hat bobbing down to one side of his plump cheeks as he waddled over behind Laramie Drake.

"*Sacre nom du nom*," he said. "It's a girl, Drake."

Drake couldn't hear any more because he had jumped across the porch and was out from under the portals, reaching the girl as she threw herself from the lathered dun. She was crying and panting and would have fallen without his support. For just that moment her red hair swept, soft and silken, across his face, and then he had recognized her.

"Midge?" he said, "what the he- . . . what are you doing here?"

She was not a large girl within the square line of her denim ducking suit, and the yellow stream of light flashed in her blue eyes as they turned up to him in a flushed, tear-stained face. "I was coming home from Tucson. Gerder stopped me where the Tanque Verde Road crosses the Old Spanish Trail. It was something about Father's papers. Gerder threatened me, even tried to get his hands on me. He cut me off from taking the trail when I got free. This was the only way left. Please, Drake, you've got to help me. Hide me or something. I don't know. . . ."

The softness of her trembling against Drake filled him with a helplessness he had never known with a woman before. "What would Gerder want with your father's papers? Why should he think you had them, anyway? Eben Hazard's been your guardian and administrator of the estate since your dad was shot in Tucson last May, hasn't he?"

"Yes, yes." Midge buried her face against his chest, drawing a labored breath as she tried to stop sobbing. "Hazard has all Dad's papers. I told you I don't know what it's about. Everything's in such a mess since Face Card's death, anyway. Gerder thinks he runs Tucson now. . . ."

"Face Card?" Drake grabbed her by the shoulders, shoving her back to stare at her face.

"Yes," she said desperately. "Your ex-partner in the Coronado House. Face Card Farrow. Murdered in his office Tuesday. I guess you know what a state that leaves Tucson in. With Face Card out, his whole machine is falling apart. The Gerder faction has stepped on the big horse and anybody who was riding Face Card Farrow's wagon had better leave this pasture. . . ." She broke off, clutching him again. "Drake, please, Drake. . . ."

The pine-crested slopes of the Tanques Verdes rose somberly against the night sky all about them with the wagon road forming a white ribbon eastward from the house and finally disappearing beneath the cottonwoods banding the dry bottoms of No Agua. It was up this road that the sound of more horses came to Drake, barely audible through the girl's hoarse breathing.

"Get that dun out of sight," he snapped at Etienne Villeneu, and grabbed the girl's elbow to shove her ahead of him into the house. For a moment her figure was silhouetted before him in the door, light catching across the maturing curve of one hip and limning the tight line of her Levi's down her slim thigh. Then he had the door shut behind them and was moving swiftly around her to an inner portal leading to Etienne's bedroom. Perhaps she hadn't expected to turn around quite so soon, because in that first instant he caught an odd calculation in her eyes. Then the fear crossed her face again, and he saw the full tremble of her lower lip above the soft curve of her chin.

"Stay in there no matter what happens," he told her, and closed the door softly after she was through. He had the gambler's instinctive suspicion of everyone, anyway, and the gambler's habitual revolt at mixing in any business not strictly his own. *Damned fool,* he told himself, frowning, and then was whirling to face the hard thunder of horses drawn to a hock-scraping halt outside and someone's drumming boots across the flagstone. The door shuddered.

"Open it," said Drake, "or did you just come to knock it down?"

Barton Gerder shoved open the heavy portal and moved into the room in a mincing suspicious, saddle-bound walk. He had a dirty-white, flat-topped hat shoved back on his big head, and his dank hair hung down over his forehead, wet with sweat, small quick eyes shifting about the room in a habitual, experienced way before they settled on Drake's broad-shouldered figure, standing, wide-legged, before the fireplace.

"Surprised you didn't have that door locked," said Gerder.

"You might shut it before the wind blows this fire out," Drake told him. "Why should I lock my doors?"

Gerder's holster sagged low enough for leather to creak softly against his dusty batwing chaps as he moved on in, wiping the dirty stubble on his strong chin as he studied Drake's sardonic face.

"Hello, Berry," said Drake.

Jack Berry, shutting the door as he came in behind Gerder, nodded to Drake, his face set in that expressionless mask Drake had become so used to in Berry's nightly visits to the faro layout at the Coronado House these last five years. He was a small, slim man, neat without being foppish in his short-skirted town coat and gray trousers tucked into plain-topped boots, giving a subtle potency to his eternal silence.

"You know why you should lock your doors, Drake," said Gerder.

"The tone of your voice would indicate this visit wasn't for friendship's sake alone," said Drake, smiling ironically.

The sarcasm brought Gerder's heavy shoulder forward, causing his soiled denim ducking jacket to fall away from the dusty front of his white shirt. "Let's not spar. I knew where the girl was headed when she turned off the Tanque Verde Road, and if you're trying to keep me from getting her, you should have locked your door."

"Girl?"

"You never were a good gambler, Drake," said Gerder, taking another mincing step forward. "You couldn't hide anything in your face. That girl ran away from her guardian, and Eben Hazard sent me to bring her back. You're bucking the law by harboring her. Fork her over and we'll forget it."

"I'm glad you put your cards on the table right away, because I can drop any misguided hospitality I might have considered and tell you to keep your whole hand right there on the edge of the table," said Drake, and the tone in his voice stopped Jack Berry abruptly from moving any farther down the room parallel to the front wall. "You're bucking the law, too, Gerder. This is armed trespass, and whatever I did about it would be justified."

The flush showed through Gerder's shadowy stubble, creeping up his thick neck and into his cheeks, but he held a restraint yet. "Drake, Face Card Farrow is dead."

Drake didn't attempt any surprise, and he saw the satisfaction in Gerder's eyes, and Berry took another step down the wall that pulled Drake up and turned him slightly toward the smaller man, and Berry stopped again.

"You should at least try and register a little astonishment," said Gerder mockingly, and then his voice hardened. "I told you, you weren't a good gambler. The girl's here, and she told you about Face Card, didn't she?"

"Did she? Berry!"

Berry stopped again, past the couch now, and Gerder's weight settled forward a little farther. "You know what Farrow's death means, Drake, better than I. As long as he held all the reins in Tucson, you could do just about as you pleased as his partner."

"I never touched Farrow's politics. My business was the Coronado House."

"As long as Farrow sat the saddle on Convent Street, you were all right. But he's out of the saddle now, Drake . . . he's let the whole bunch of reins go, and the horses are running wild. You don't hold so much as the toe of your boot in Tucson's poke now. Sheriff Kennedy is just one example. Farrow's man? Everybody knew it. Just a matter of time now before Kennedy vacates his office, voluntarily or involuntarily. He's afraid to make a move in any direction. The law's through backing any play you make. You aren't safe even out here in your prairie-dog hole. Farrow made as many enemies as friends, and you were his partner, Drake, and they aren't going to discriminate."

"Move your cards closer."

"You can see my cards . . . you know what I'm driving at." Gerder lowered his head a little, staring at Drake from beneath his dark brow. "You're blocked on every side, Drake, you're not in a position to buck anybody. And that goes for me. You're in a deeper hole than the sheriff, being Farrow's partner. Any way you jump is into the fire."

"I *was* Farrow's partner," said Drake. "The petition to dissolve our association has been in the court's hands for a week."

"That won't make any difference," said Gerder. "You know it. I'm only trying to show you why you'd better hand over Midge Lawrence without a ruckus, Drake. You aren't in any position to make me take her by force. You have no recourse, no matter what I do here."

"Haven't I?" said Drake.

"You know what I mean."

"And you know what I mean."

Gerder's quick eyes dropped from Drake's lean face to the strap across his shoulder holding the Knuckle Duster underneath his armpit; it wasn't a very heavy strap, hardly noticeable to a man who didn't know what it meant, for the Reid wasn't a large gun, being only three inches overall and meant for a pocket hide-out, where most men carried it, but Drake preferred the armpit so he could pack it when his coat was off, and Gerder knew what it meant, and what Drake meant.

"Drake," said Gerder, and took a heavy breath, "you're in a big enough tight already without going about things this here way."

"Berry," snapped Drake, "I warn you. . . ."

But Jack Berry kept on moving toward the big desk in the corner of the room, and Drake understood how his target was already too separated, and how Gerder's whole body was settling on down that way, and his voice suddenly cut savagely at them.

"All right, go ahead, damn you, go ahead. . . ."

"Drake, I think I won't have that Filets of Hare after all. I think *Timbale de foie gras Montesque* is . . ."

"Berry!" shouted Gerder, and went for his gun.

It had all come at once like that but Drake had already picked his man, knowing he had to take one or the other with them that far apart, and he was fading toward Jack Berry because he had pegged him as the fastest. But the hollow thump came hard on Gerder's shout, and Drake saw Berry stiffen, thrown back against the wall by the motion of his own body, and a big carving knife quivered in the adobe not an inch from Berry's right ear, and he stood rigid there without trying to get his gun out any farther. Almost before he had turned toward Berry, Drake was whirling back to Gerder, maybe it was this that stopped Gerder, or maybe Gerder had stopped already. The big sweating man was bent forward in his crouch, and his gun was not any farther from its holster than Berry's.

"Go ahead," said Drake. "I want you to, Gerder. Go on."

Gerder's eyes were on Drake's hand where it was held stiffly out in front of the gambler's white shirt front, thumb cocked up and taut fingers pointing outward. Gerder remained in his crouch a moment longer, then his hoarse inhalation seemed to draw him up in a series of spasmodic jerks, his grimy hand lifting carefully the black rubber grip of his Colt.

Berry had relaxed somewhat, but was still against the wall that way, and Drake saw what had held him from further movement. Etienne Villeneu stood in the kitchen door, holding his other carving knife by its tip. His twinkling eyes shifted slyly in their fat pouches from Berry to Gerder to Drake, and then he chuckled, and tossed the knife into the air a little so he could catch it by the hilt and spat upon the whetstone in his other hand.

"As I was saying," he grinned, beginning to hone the blade, "I think *Timbale de foie gras Montesque* would be better for a Tuesday night. I think Hungarian sauce would be indicated here, too." He looked up, raising his eyebrows. "What do you think, *M'sieu* Gerder?"

Gerder did not answer, standing there staring at Drake, his jaw shoved out and lower lip working

111

at his upper in a habitual, frustrated way. Drake had held that hand cocked out in front of him until now, and he lowered it with an ironic smile. "Would it be impolite of me to ask that you leave now?"

Gerder inclined his head toward Berry, and the smaller man moved away from the wall so he would have room to pass the long knife sticking out of the adobe, and then slid down the wall to the door, opening it, still facing toward Drake. Gerder started to back out after Berry, then stopped again.

"You've just built yourself a wooden suit, Drake," he said between set teeth. "It isn't only the girl. Part of it's her, but that's just the start. It isn't only the set-up in Tucson, either. That's another part, too, but that don't begin to cover it. I'll tell you what does cover it, Drake. The suit I mentioned. The kind you wear when they put you in that six-foot hole in the ground. You've built it all yourself, Drake, and all you have to do now is put it on."

II

It was June and the slopes of the Tanques Verdes were lush with Texas crab and blue gramma grass, and higher up the Ponderosa pine mingled its darksome beauty with the lighter ash that marched

112

down off the crests, and every morning before dawn Laramie Drake had arisen like this and gone out in a heavy Mackinaw to stand in the meadow before his new house and watch the sun come up over the eastward ridges. It was new to him, getting up that early, and it was new to him, calling such land his own, and it was good to him somehow. It was only at night that he felt a restless longing for the old life, but when the sun cast its first pink light over the spread of his meadows this way, he forgot the lure of smoky saloons and green-topped tables and stacked chips and women with their dresses cut low across white bosoms to attract a man's eye and the endless call of keno dealers and roulette croupiers. For the moment, standing here on the porch, he had forgotten Gerder, and the night before, but as the door opened, he turned nervously and realized it had been at the back of his mind all the time.

"What do you want for breakfast," Etienne said. "*Melon cantaloupe glace? Oeufs-sur-le-Plat?*"

"Eggs on a dish . . . eggs anyway." Drake moved his dark head impatiently. "Villey, what are we going to do with that girl?"

"Midge?" Etienne's eyebrows rose. "Why do anything with her? She seems to like it here. You need a woman around."

"Don't be absurd. I'll just get into trouble keeping her here. When I mentioned taking her back to Hazard last night, she went all to pieces. What have they been doing to her, Villey? A girl should trust her guardian, at least." He became aware that Midge had come up behind Villeneu and felt a faint flush creep into his face, as if he had been caught at something to be ashamed of, and then knew an anger at himself for that. "Why is it, Midge? What's wrong with Hazard?"

Etienne moved away from the door, and she stood with one hand on the frame, not meeting his eyes. "I don't know, Drake. I'm afraid of him. He has such a temper. He's always prying at me, implying I'm hiding some of Dad's things or something. I have a big fight with him every time I even want to leave the house. It's like a prison."

He sensed there was more to it than that. "You never did get along with Eben, did you? I remember last May you were worrying Judge Petrie about getting another administrator."

"I guess I've caused the judge a lot of trouble," she said. "Caused everybody a lot . . ."

"Don't take that attitude," he said. "You know we all want to help you in any way we can. Can't you tell me a little more of what it was about last night? Gerder said he had come from Hazard to get you. That doesn't jibe with your story."

Her lustrous red hair bobbed at her neck with the sharp upward tilt of her head. "You don't believe . . . ?"

"I believe you."

"Then maybe Gerder *is* working with Hazard," she said. "How do we know where anybody stands, with this upset in Tucson. Hazard was mixed up in Farrow's politics just as much as anybody. Hazard's chairman of the Tucson Cattlemen's Association, and half the men in the T.C.A. were under Farrow's thumb, one way or another. Gerder wouldn't tell me straight out what he wanted last night. He seemed to think I knew well enough. He said it affected everybody in the Tanques Verdes, everybody in Tucson, for that matter. Please, Drake, don't make me go back to Hazard."

"I can't keep you here, Midge. You'd better get ready."

She turned from the door abruptly, and he saw her shoulders trembling as she moved back toward the room she had slept in. He turned toward Etienne, holding out a helpless hand.

"What can I do, Villey? I've got to take her back. I wouldn't know how to treat a girl like that. When she's around, I feel so . . . ," he hesitated, not knowing exactly how he felt, hunting for the word with another vague motion of his hand.

Etienne laughed slyly. "That sounds funny coming from you. I never saw you at a loss with a woman before, Drake."

Eben Hazard's Lazy Hook spread skirted the eastern edge of Tucson just north of the Old

Spanish Trail, the sprawling adobe house and large pack pole corrals set in a hollow of foothills whose low cactus-studded crests overlooked the town. Midge Lawrence rode her jaded dun sullenly beside Drake on his stockinged black as they cantered down the rutted wagon trace, Etienne bringing up the rear on an outrageously fat albino. Drake saw the Lazy Hook hands gathering in a little bunch across the pattern of pack poles formed by the first corral, and he sat a little straighter on his horse, feeling the first tension in him. Gerder? Maybe. Or maybe the trouble in Tucson. Who knew?

Over the plod of the horses as they slowed to a trot came the sudden hard drum of boots, and Drake saw Eben Hazard running from the house toward the corral at a hard jog, shouting at them: "Midge! Midge, where have you been? I was worried sick. . . ."

Then he must have seen who rode beside her, because he slowed down, and he was walking as he reached the other men at the corral, and then stopped. Eben Hazard was a large, florid man, the pure white shock of hair accentuating the ruddy flush in heavy cheeks that might have come from sun or drink, or both, and he stood with his expensive Justins spread widely apart to support the solid bulk of his thick torso. Drake halted his horse and managed to keep his black from turning toward Hazard as he stepped off.

"Gerder in your string again, Eben?"

Hazard's answer came spontaneously enough, but his heavy, vibrant voice had a sullen sound. "I haven't seen Bart Gerder since I found him writing a wrong tally up in my brand book three years ago. How is it you're with Midge?"

"She hit my spread last night," said Drake, glancing at the girl where she sat stiffly on her dun, her chin up so her eyes met neither his nor Hazard's. "Running from Gerder. She said he wanted something of her father's. Cut her off from heading this way when she got away."

Drake was watching Hazard's reaction but could ascertain nothing from it as the heavy man stiffened, glancing sharply up at the girl. "I told you not to get that far from home while this mess was going on, Midge. Gerder's bunch is running wild now that Farrow's grip is off the town. They've been held down so long by Farrow there's no telling what will happen." He tried to soften his voice. "Never mind, honey, it's all over now. You just get down and we'll give you a good hot meal and keep you here."

Drake saw the way she pulled away, muttering: "I've had a good hot meal. I'm not staying here, Eben, I can't. I'm going to get a room in town. Let me go, Eben."

"Don't be a little fool, Midge, you can't go into town. That's the most dangerous place for you now. You're not of age and you're under my

117

protection and you'll do as I say. Get off that dun"—he tried to catch her by the waist with both hands and pull her to one side so he could lift her off bodily—"get off now. I'm losing my patience with you."

"Hold your hand, Eben," said Drake, catching at the man's arm. "She isn't one of your balky mules."

"Stay out of this, Drake!" shouted Hazard, his face almost purple with rage now, jerking at Drake's grasp. "She's my ward, and I'll handle her the way I think best. She's a willful, stubborn, foolish little girl, and she has to be taught a lesson. Running off to your place like that. It ought to show you. Why didn't she come to me? That would have been the proper thing. No, she has to run off to a gambler's house . . . a bachelor's house at that."

"That doesn't give you the right to pull her around," said Drake, yanking at him again as the heavy man tried to get Midge off. She was half out of her saddle, fighting and kicking to get free, blazing anger in her eyes.

"Let go, Drake." Hazard suddenly turned toward his men, who had spread away from the corral around the horses. "Kirkboot, get this man off me!"

Kirkboot was only a step away from Drake. He was Hazard's foreman, a big ugly man with a broken nose. A couple of other hands shifted with him as he took that first step to get Drake, and then they all stopped, looking up past Drake in a surprised way.

"I have here," said Etienne Villeneu from the fat back of his albino horse, "a French LeMat. In the cylinder are nine Thirty-Eight-caliber revolver bullets for the upper barrel, and serving as a base pin for the cylinder is a twenty-eight-gauge shotgun barrel. There is a movable firing pin on the hammer for either the upper barrel or the lower, and if any of you men wish to test the efficiency of this singular weapon, you might tell me which load you would prefer, a Thirty-Eight slug, or the buckshot, and I would be glad to adjust the firing accordingly."

It held the other men there, but Hazard had not quit trying to get Midge down, and she lost her balance suddenly and fell off onto him, and he stumbled back with her weight into Drake. Crying now in her anger, Midge fought at Hazard, trying to get free of him. He caught at her arm to keep from being mauled, and she cried aloud with the pain of his grip, pulling her arm up sharply to bite his hand.

"Damn you!" he roared, and Drake saw his heavy, hairy hand come back, and tried to stop it and couldn't.

Midge staggered back against her dun from the blow, and the pain was still in her twisted face as Drake jumped Hazard, catching him by the shoulder and whirling him around, putting all his hundred and seventy pounds into the punch. Hazard's feet left the ground as he went backward, and then struck again, and the spike heels plowed two furrows before he went over onto his back. Drake had time to see the others running in among the three spooked horses to put the animals between them and Etienne, and one of the men had a dally he snaked out in a neat hooley-ann and that caught the Frenchman as his first shot exploded, snagging him sideways off his albino. Then Drake was whirling to meet Kirkboot and his two men. He staggered back under the impact of the foreman's heavy body crashing into him, rolling a bony fist off his shoulder before it caught his face.

He knew it would unbalance him, but there were three of them, and it was the only way he could hope to get one out of the fight before they were all on him. Still going backward, he let one knee come up. He heard Kirkboot grunt sickly as the knee caught him, and when Drake went down, the foreman's weight came helplessly with him. Drake was twisting from beneath the man even before he hit, and was out from beneath Kirkboot, rolling away from the other two men, and when he finally came to his feet again, Kirkboot was still huddled on the ground, his hands underneath him, moaning.

The other pair had come in a blind rush,

meaning to hit Drake before he was in position, but he put his fist out while he was still crouched with rising, and the shock of the first man ramming into it almost knocked his shoulder out of joint. He jerked aside to let the man stumble on past with the blood already covering his face from a smashed nose, and threw himself in under the second one's cocked arms to get his shoulder in the belly and heave. The man's own momentum carried him over Drake's back and he landed on the top of his head with a sodden, cracking sound that brought a strangled scream from him. The other Lazy Hook hand was turning around in a fumbling way and pawing the blood out of his face so he could find Drake, but Drake saw what Hazard was doing, and jumped forward away from that last man.

Eben Hazard had grabbed a stirrup leather on Midge's frightened, rearing dun to pull himself erect, and must have only gotten fully to his feet when the men had struck Drake, because he had just now let go the leather and taken a vicious step forward, going for his gun. Jumping away from that man toward Hazard, it was a spasmodic reaction for Drake's hand to shoot out that way, thumb cocked up, and slap down for his Knuckle Duster. His fingers were under the torn lapel of his coat before he stopped himself. Hazard was still fumbling to draw, his big Peacemaker not yet out of leather.

Going on forward in his jump, Drake shouted something he didn't recognize himself and pulled his hand from beneath his coat empty. His body slamming into Hazard knocked the man back against the rump of the dun, and with one hand he grasped the man's gun wrist, preventing it from pulling the Peacemaker quite free of the holster, and the gun exploded toward the ground, jarring up against Drake's grasp.

"I told you dirty *paillards*!" Drake heard Etienne shouting from somewhere on the other side of the whinnying rearing horses, "a flock of Twenty-Eight gauge for your Fricandeau." The explosion of his LeMat drowned out whatever else he yelled.

"Drake!" cried Hazard brokenly—"Drake!"—and then Drake's free fist struck his face, knocking him back against the side-stepping dun.

"Not the same as fighting with a girl, is it, Eben," snarled Drake, and hit him again.

"Drake!" choked Hazard once more, trying to jerk his Peacemaker free. Drake pulled it clear of leather for him, then twisted the man's thick wrist till Hazard made a strangled sound of pain and dropped the gun. The dun was clear away now, breaking for the corral with the spooked albino and the black, and when Drake put his fist into Hazard's face for the fourth time, he felt Hazard jerk back with nothing behind him and released the man so the blow could knock him completely over.

Swaying there above the owner of the Lazy Hook, panting, his lip bleeding, Drake could see the others. Etienne crouched on one knee on the other side of the spot where the horses had been, the dally rope still hanging around his neck and under one armpit, the smoking LeMat in his pudgy hand. The Lazy Hook man who had thrown the dally lay holding a leg soaked with blood the way it seeps from a buckshot wound, and two others stood farther back, staring sullenly at the gun in the Frenchman's fist. Kirkboot still lay on his belly, along with the man Drake had thrown over his shoulder, and the man with the bloody face had apparently decided he wouldn't try anything else alone. It was Midge finally, moving from where she had stumbled when Hazard had shoved her away from the spooked dun. Her eyes traveled from Hazard, on the ground, to Drake, and there was surprise in her voice more than anything.

"You didn't kill him," she said.

III

The Indian name for the town had been Stjukshon, which meant Dark Springs, and Padre Eusebio Kino was the first man to see it, building the mission of San Xavier del Bac to the south of the Indian village, which he had named San Cosme

123

del Tucson. Much of the Old Town, or El Barrio Libre, as the Mexicans called that neighborhood inhabited mostly by Negroes and Indians, was still formed of the same adobe hovels that Kino had seen in the 17th Century, but farther north on Meyer Street the dilapidated adobes gave way to new frame houses. The eastern portion of Tucson, around Plaza Militar, had been quiet enough, when Drake and Etienne and the girl rode in, but now as they entered West Corral from Scott, the clamor began to reach them. A pair of seraped Mexicans halted on the corner in the shadows of a low adobe, one of them motioning toward Drake, and from across the street a man called softly to someone within a *cantina*, and a Papago Indian and a bearded white man moved out of the dark door to stare.

"You're crazy to come in here now, Laramie," said Etienne. "Already they begin to pass the word. Every man on Convent will know you're coming before you even reach the Coronado."

Drake was stiff and sore from the fight, angry at himself for getting sucked into this. "Never mind. What did you mean back at the Lazy Hook when you said I didn't kill him, Midge?"

There was a speculation in her eyes, studying him, and she smiled a little, shrugging. "You had your hand on your gun."

"You said it as if you expected me to kill him."

She shrugged again, not answering, and Etienne

chuckled. "I think she has been hearing too many stories about you, Drake. You would be surprised, *ma'm'selle*, how rarely Drake does use that Knuckle Duster of his."

"But Hazard went for his gun first," said Midge. "He fully intended shooting you while you were taken up with fighting those other men. It would have been self-defense. You even had your hand on your gun. Any other man would have shot him."

"If you had known Drake as long as I have known him, perhaps you would understand a little better," said Etienne. "There are some gamblers who use a marked deck, and others who play a straight game. It would have looked like self-defense, perhaps, to us, and to the Lazy Hook hands, and there would be no one to say Drake dealt any cards from the bottom, but maybe Drake knew it wouldn't really have been self-defense"—Etienne tapped his heart—"in here. You saw the way Hazard was getting that gun. He hadn't even cleared leather by the time Drake reached him."

There was still that speculation in Midge's eyes, watching Drake, and his own irritation drove him to it. "Next time I'll shoot the man, if that'll make you happier."

"Drake, don't talk that way," she murmured. "I realize you're angry with me for all the trouble I've caused. This is just going to make you madder. I went to Judge Petrie a couple of months ago, and he wouldn't help. Hazard's too big a man for Petrie to antagonize by appointing another guardian for me."

"Naturally Petrie didn't want to put in the petition himself," said Drake. "It's his own court that grants the appeal. But he's been my friend ever since I hit this town, and my putting in the appeal will take the responsibility off his shoulders." He turned on her abruptly. "And then I'm through, understand. I'll put in the appeal and see that it's carried through and get you a man who can take care of you right. Then I'm through."

"You don't need to sound so angry about it. If you feel that way, why did you even bother to take me away from the Lazy Hook this afternoon?"

"I can't see any man treating a kid like that."

"I'm not a kid."

"Let's forget it. I don't know why I should feel responsible for you, but . . ."—his head turned toward the sound of boots hard heeling it up Corral away from them—"wasn't that Jack, Etienne?"

"Berry?" said Etienne. "Looks like him from the posterior. *Voila*! It would seem Barton Gerder is setting up competition for the Coronado House."

The running man had crossed the intersection of Corral and Convent and shoved through the

126

batwing doors of the old Aces Up. There was a new sign above the façade, however. Gerder's Saloon. The hubbub ahead of them grew as they neared the intersection. The sidewalk rattled under a man's running feet, and he appeared around the end of the corner building, turning down Corral as the first shot clipped splinters from the sidewalk just behind him. His boots stirred the hot dust laying thickly over the plank walk, and it sifted up, dry and fetid, into Drake's nostrils, and then a second man reeled around the corner, firing again, and the acrid odor of powder smoke mingled with that of the dust. The first man ducked into an adobe *tienda*, and the drunk with the gun emptied his weapon, knocking scarlet *ristras* of chiles off the *viga* poles.

A bartender showed at the corner, running after the drunk. "Garcia," he shouted, "put that gun down, Garcia . . . !"

From behind him, Drake heard the clatter of wheels and the whooping of men. He caught at Midge's bridle and forced her over into the curb as a livery wagon careened by them, bouncing through the wheel ruts, surrounded by half a dozen cowhands yelling at the frightened livery horses and turning their own ponies into the wagon, trying to tip it over. Drake reached the hitch rack in front of the Coronado House on the northwest corner of Corral and Convent, and as he stepped off his horse and dropped the reins on the cottonwood rail, he caught sight of the men gathering on the plank walk beneath the wooden overhang of Gerder's Saloon on the southeast corner of the same intersection. The cowboys had turned the wagon over on down Corral, and the frightened driver was running back up the street, hazed by the whooping men, and the bartender and two bouncers were struggling with the drunk across the way, and all that noise only seemed to accentuate the silence of the men in front of Gerder's.

"*Oui*," said Etienne, "that was Jack Berry."

"And Gerder." Drake's voice was hardly audible. Then he turned to Etienne, speaking louder: "Stay at the door, Etienne, and let me know if Gerder makes any move."

The Coronado House had the usual crowd around the doors. Drake recognized most of them. Several rose from where they had been sitting in the deep sills of the windows flanking the doors, and the others moved out of Drake's way, something sullen in the way they watched him as he helped Midge up the high curb.

" 'Morning, Chad," he said.

The banker's son took out a cheroot and engaged himself in lighting it without raising his eyes to Drake. The gambler looked at several others he knew, and their glance was somewhere else. Shrugging, he shoved through the near pair of batwings, and heard Etienne follow him in and stop the doors from swinging and turn around to face the street. A dark man with his hair parted in the middle and plastered down, stood at the bar, the tails of his black cutaway whipping at his legs as he saw Drake in the gold-framed back-bar mirror and whirled, and though there was not much expression on his face, Drake saw how it was here, too, and he began to realize how big a mistake he had made in bringing Midge to town. He felt like a man standing on sand that was rapidly slipping out from beneath him. He had expected some friends, at least, to remain. Enough, at least, to nullify whatever move Gerder might make long enough for Drake to get this over with.

"Hello, Keno," he said. "Sort of a surprise, finding Gerder established right across the street. Is that why you won't shake hands?"

The dark man had come reluctantly across the room, meeting Drake's eyes with some effort. "Things have changed, Drake. . . ."

"So have my friends," said Drake. "I thought you'd have the guts to buck Gerder at least."

"It's sort of awkward, Drake. . . ."

"Having me here, you mean? Afraid Gerder might take offense? Where's Colorado? Or is he even afraid to meet me?"

Another man had come over from the bar. He was slope-shouldered and thick-set and must have been able to slip his starched white choke-collars on over his head. He bit a cold black stogie into one corner of thick lips and his derby hat was pulled so low Drake could hardly find his eyes.

"Albert Binder," he said, and Drake got the idea he was introducing himself. "Drake? Glad to find you. Been hunting some time. Like to talk."

"I don't have time right now," said Drake.

"Represent Pacific Railroad Corporation," said the man, biting at his words the way he did his cigar. "Building their spur line from Santa Fe now and want the right of way on Apache Gap. Only way through the Tanques Verdes. Otherwise have to lay about two hundred extra miles of track around the northwest corner of the Verdes to reach Tucson."

"I asked you where Colorado was," Drake said to Keno.

"So they're willing to offer a goodly sum to save them doing that. . . ."

"Colorado disappeared a couple of days ago with the house owing him two weeks back pay," said Keno, glancing at Binder enigmatically. "It seemed queer at the time."

"Am I to take it you don't think he left of his own volition?"

"It isn't like Colorado to leave that much money behind," said Keno.

"Gerder?"

Something passed through Keno's imperturbable eyes. "Who knows? Who knows anything in this town now? Gerder moved in across the street as soon as he heard Face Card was dead. Took half our business. What he couldn't get with cut-throat prices he practically forced over at the point of a gun."

"I don't see Judge Petrie around," said Drake. "He used to eat lunch here about this time."

"We've been serving Petrie's lunch to him in Face Card's office while he went through Face Card's papers. The court took over till you could get in."

"Who killed Face Card?"

Keno's voice held a growing withdrawal. "Farrow was smoked out in the office about two in the morning. There was too much noise going on at the gambling tables to hear the shot. We found him the next morning, sitting at the desk with his face shot off, all his papers scattered over the room. Petrie's had a time putting them together again."

Drake touched Midge's elbow, meaning to move her down the bar toward the stairway at the rear of the house, but Binder got in their way again.

"Guess you didn't understand. I represent Pacific . . ."

"I guess *you* didn't understand," said Drake, and the sweep of his arm caught the stocky man across his chest and sent him crashing up against one of the tables on the other side. Without looking back at him, Drake guided Midge through the tables of the front dining room, separated from the gambling hall by a low broad-topped rail covered with buttoned crimson plush.

Near the arched entrance into the gambling hall, a black-haired woman stood with her back against the bar, her elbows up on the mahogany, the soft light from the glass chandelier drinking in the rich wine of her gown and glittering across the jade buttons on her elbow-length suede gloves. Silently, as Drake passed, she removed one elbow from the bar and reached for her drink, raising it to him. Over the rim of the glass, her smoldering black eyes met his, and his thin lips worked into a faint, ironic smile.

"Donna," he said.

"Drake," she said, and took the drink.

With his hand still touching Midge's elbow, he could feel the distinct stiffening of her body. They were past the woman now, and he turned a little to see how Midge's chin had lifted.

"She's an exotic woman," said Midge.

Their boots echoed across the polished floor of the big gambling hall. "Where did you learn that word?"

She looked into his face abruptly, the smile there bringing a flush to her cheeks. "Do you know her very well?"

"Very well."

They passed a bored croupier leaning on his roulette table with a beer and a plate of pretzels, nodding at Drake, and the girl took a careful breath. "I imagine you've known many women . . . very well."

"Do you?" he said, and took a last look toward the front door as they mounted the carpeted stairs. Keno had come up to Donna at the bar, and both of them were looking after Drake, with something different in each of their faces, and Etienne's broad fat back blocked off one set of batwings. "I think it would behoove us to get this over as quickly as possible. Keno's got some bouncers, but Gerder might want you bad enough to take that chance."

IV

Face Card Farrow's office overlooked Corral Street, light from its two bay windows spilling into the sumptuous room with an inch-thick nap on the carpet and several ponderous Gothic armchairs facing a huge Chippendale desk squatting on claw feet beneath a copy of Goya's Nude Duchess. Judge Oliver Petrie was sitting behind the desk, his white head bent over a motley collection of papers and legal documents, a half-eaten lunch on the silver tray at his elbow. He looked up as Drake ushered Midge in, and it was surprise on his seamed, worried face at first, and then something else Drake didn't want to define.

"Laramie," he said, and his smile didn't stay on

133

very long. He waved a gnarled hand at the papers. "I'm glad you've come, in a way, and sorry in another. Face Card's papers have to be taken care of, but this town's no place for you right now. Farrow's whole machine fell apart with his death, and every enemy he made is riding the high horse now. You saw Gerder's saloon. When he finds you have the papers . . ."

"But I didn't come here for the papers."

"They're yours, Drake." Petrie's surprise seemed genuine. "You know how Farrow was fighting to keep you from pulling out. I think he was afraid you knew too much."

"I didn't know anything. I never touched his politics. If he wanted to mess in that end, I didn't mind, but I kept my cards down on the poker tables. . . ."

"Face Card had a petition in the courts restraining you from dissolving the partnership until you'd settled your own personal debts to the firm's satisfaction. It took the court several weeks to find those claims of your debts were erroneous, and we hadn't yet refused the petition when Face Card was killed."

"His death dissolves the partnership automatically."

"Yes," said Petrie, "but as you were technically still his partner at the time of death, and as he has no living relatives in evidence, his estate falls to you. I don't care what you do with the Coronado

House or the other liquid assets . . . sell it to Keno, if you want, or even Gerder . . . I don't care. But you've got to help me with Farrow's papers, Drake. They're dynamite. Not the actual documents we have here, but the possession of them. A lot of them are gone. Obviously the reason he was killed. He was found with the papers all over the room. I know, for instance . . . though I could never do anything about it . . . that Face Card had a signed confession from Jack Berry admitting the killing of Pablo Señora in Prescott in 'Ninety-Seven. You remember what a big smell that business caused. Farrow's possession of that confession was one reason he could hold Gerder down so tight, Gerder and Berry being such close cronies. That paper is gone. One of the things that leads me to believe there are a number of other papers missing. The same type of papers. Things which gave Farrow his control over so many men."

"You think Gerder . . . ?"

"I don't know," said Petrie. "All I'm trying to show you is the significance of these papers. Everybody knows they contained evidence enough to send half the men in Tucson to jail, and it must be rather obvious to everyone that Farrow was killed by some man he had been blackmailing, in order to destroy the evidence. But they don't know which papers were taken and which weren't. If it wasn't Gerder, for instance, who shot Farrow, then Gerder would have no way of knowing whether that confession of Berry's was destroyed, or still in evidence, and he would do a lot to try and gain it if he thought it was in a position to damage him."

"You're saying that whoever holds those papers is a target for all the men Farrow was blackmailing, no matter whether the stuff he used to control them is still there or not," said Drake. "All right. What can I do?"

"Take the papers," said Petrie. "They're your legal property, along with everything else. There are still a few things left among them we can use against some of the men I've been waiting to nail a long time, but we'll have to wait till things settle down in Tucson, and we have some kind of law to back up whatever move the courts make. Sheriff Kennedy was Farrow's man, and he's afraid to show his nose out his office door now. The town marshal was shot up in a street fight last week."

"All right," said Drake. "I'll take the papers off your hands, even announce publicly that I have them, if you'll do something for me. I tried to tell you I came here for Midge. How did you ever pick Eben Hazard for her guardian?"

"What do you mean?" Petrie's voice held something defensive. "I didn't pick him. He's her uncle, the nearest living relative."

"He's no man to raise a kid like Midge. When I

brought her back this morning, he yanked her around like she was a honky-tonk girl and knocked her down. I have an idea that isn't the first time."

Petrie pursed his lips, waved a deprecatory hand. "Surely you can't mean that, Drake. Perhaps he just lost his temper. She's a"—he glanced at Midge—"a rather stubborn child. I know by experience."

"Stubborn or not, no man has a right to knock her around like that," said Drake. "I thought she was exaggerating things till I saw that this morning. I knew Hazard had a mean temper, but I didn't think he was the kind to take it out on a kid. . . ."

"I'm not a kid," said Midge hotly.

The right-hand window was open halfway, and Drake became aware of utter silence in Corral Street below. It was ominous, somehow, after the clamor. He stepped to the desk, grabbing the carved edge with both hands.

"Listen, Oliver, something's started down there. Are you going to get a new guardian for Midge, or aren't you? I'm not taking her back to Hazard. She's in some kind of trouble. Gerder's after her for something he thinks her father had. It might even be mixed in with this business about Face Card Farrow. She needs someone capable of protecting her and treating her like a human being."

Petrie looked at the desk. "Hazard's chairman of the Tucson Cattlemen's Association, Drake. They're about the only hope the law-abiding citizens have left in this town. We can't afford to offend him now . . . we're in a bad enough tight without lining up any more against us. . . ."

"I guess I should have seen it before." Drake's voice was bitter, because he had considered this man his friend. "You're quite willing to put me on the spot handing me those papers, but you don't want to take any cards in the game yourself."

"They're your legal responsibility. . . ."

"And it's your legal responsibility to see that Midge Lawrence is properly taken care of. Are you going to do it, Oliver, or am I going to take it to a federal court? That wouldn't put you in a nice light, you know."

"Now, Drake, you're in no position to make any move like that. You'd better take Midge right back to Hazard, or you'll find yourself subpoenaed for abduction of a minor. You know I'm your friend, and I'd do anything I could, but we're just up against something bigger than us. . . ."

The door rattled to someone's knock, and then the croupier pushed in without invitation, still eating his pretzels. "Keno sent me up, Drake. Gerder's started across the street. He's got a big bunch, and it looks like business."

"It's the papers!" cried Petrie. "He knows I'm up here with Farrow's papers. . . ."

"Don't be a fool, it's Midge he wants!" Drake turned to the croupier. "Tell Etienne to come on up. We'll take the back way out." Petrie tried to get around the desk and past Drake, but the gambler caught him by the lapel. "Oliver, are you going to put through a petition for another guardian?"

"Drake, I told you . . ."

"All right." There was something final in Drake's voice, and he turned toward the desk, scooping up Judge Petrie's big leather case to begin stuffing papers into the pockets. "Petrie, you dealt this hand. Whatever happens from here on out, just remember that. You dealt it. You want me to take Farrow's papers? You're damned right I will. If you don't have the guts to use them, I will. You think Tucson's in a mess now. You don't know what a mess looks like. I'll put on so much pressure that Corral Street will come apart at the seams. They don't know what I do have here, and what I don't have, and when I start the squeeze, you'll be surprised at the men that pop out of the war sack. It doesn't matter if most of the evidence was taken. It's as good a way to find out who murdered Face Card Farrow as any. Find the man who doesn't jump when I threaten him with this, and you'll have the killer. If it wasn't Hazard who killed Farrow, I won't need a federal court to make him move. I'll have Eben himself putting in the petition for another guardian for Midge. Now get out of my way."

Shoving Midge ahead of him, he brushed past the pale judge and out the door. Etienne waited at the bottom of the stairs, his LeMat in his hand. As Drake ran down the stairs, Donna Claire came from beneath them where the hall led to the back door. He saw the look on her face and didn't need any more.

"About a dozen of them, Drake. They ran a linchpin wagon across the end of the alley. You wouldn't stand a chance of getting out the back way. Gerder even has some men across Corral, watching the windows on that side." She came in close, ignoring Midge to catch at his arm, looking up into his face. "Drake . . ."

"It's all right, Donna," he said. "How about the front, Villey?"

"They already got our horses," said Etienne, twirling his waxed mustache. "Keno has some bouncers behind the batwings. I don't know how long that will last."

Drake moved toward the front, shoving the briefcase into Etienne's hands. "We've got to get out some way. It might as well be the front door. If anything happens to me, Villey, get that briefcase to the marshal's office at Prescott."

"If anything happens to you, Laramie," said Etienne, "it will happen to me, also."

"Drake . . ." Midge clutched at his arm, following him so close she bumped against him, tripping on his feet. "I'm going with you. Don't leave me."

"Don't worry, honey." He had one arm around her shoulder, half running through the gilded archway, calling to the bartender. "Henry, how about that Greener?"

Henry was standing with one red, hammy hand on the polished mahogany, looking through the front windows. He reached beneath the bar without speaking and came up with a scatter-gun, tossing it to Drake. The gambler took his arm off Midge's slender shoulders to catch the sawed-off weapon deftly, and then he stepped around in front of her.

"Keep in close behind me," he said. "I never saw a scatter-gun yet that wouldn't stop a crowd."

He did not know who had gotten in his way till the man began to speak in that toneless, mechanical voice. "Don't be a fool. That crowd's after you. Don't be a fool, Drake. Out for blood. Now P.R. is willing to pay you . . ."

"Did I ever tell you how I made *Filets le Levraut a la Mornay*, *M'sieu* Pacific Railroads," said Etienne, pushing his LeMat in between Drake and Binder, and gently shoving the short man backward with the flat of its barrel. "First I trim the filets of two leverets, *compre*? Then I cut the filets into slices, one-inch diameter and one-third inch thick . . ."

Drake had moved on past by then, and Keno's heavy-shouldered bouncer was the only man left between him and the batwings. "How about it, Sam?"

Sam Marshal moved away from the doors, shaking his head. "I wouldn't try it Drake. I've bucked a lot of crowds in my time, and it's the quiet ones that are the worst. If I hadn't been watching all the time, I wouldn't know this bunch was out there. I wouldn't try to do a darned . . ."

The hot suffocation of the dust was the first thing that struck Drake as he stepped through the slatted doors. There might have been a dozen men in Gerder's crowd, shifting in toward the empty sidewalk in front of the Coronado House. A short ugly man in a black hat and a loud vest had taken the reins of the three horses off the rack, and Jack Berry and Barton Gerder and three or four others were already on this side of the rack, mounting the curb. None of them had drawn guns yet, but when the batwings popped open before Drake, Gerder stopped with one foot on the high plank walk, and Drake saw his shoulder rise, and those of several others.

"Don't do it, Bart," said Drake, moving out into the shadow beneath the overhang. The bunched muscles of his jaw drew that odd scar pattern taut across his high cheek bone. "I've got a pair of twelve gauges in this Greener that will blow the belly right out of the first man who gets his iron free, and I can see every one of you."

Gerder took his foot off the walk as Drake came out. "You'll never make it, Drake. Corral's full of my men from Meyer to Convent. That scatter-gun won't blast you out."

"This scatter-gun will take anybody to hell with me that wants to go," said Drake. "Keep moving back, Bart. Drop those reins, Italy."

"Keep moving those nags out, Italy," snarled Gerder.

The man in the loud vest looked from Gerder to Drake's Greener, and dropped the reins. "You want these nags moved out, Gerder, you'll have to do it yourself."

"Close to me, kid," muttered Drake as he felt Midge's hands, small and soft, hanging onto his coat, her body bumping up against him with every other step as he moved across the walk, swinging the scatter-gun slowly from right to left. He had seen the threat of a shotgun control a crowd when nothing else would, and it was doing that now. There was no fear in Gerder's face, but he backed out into the street. There was fear in the faces of the others, and they spread away, too. The sunlight struck Drake a hot blow as he stepped from the shade beneath the overhang and stood on the edge of the curb. He was reluctant to lose what-ever advantage this height gave him, and he let the Greener swing toward Italy again. "Now bring them in here."

Sweat greased Italy's face as he got the reins again and led the horses into the curb. The men shifted restlessly out in the sun, and Drake felt the first impatience rake his loins with its small claws, and tried to down it, knowing what a mistake that would be. Yet he couldn't help wondering how much longer they would hold out there. Gerder's jaw was sticking out, lower lip working across his upper that way, and Drake could see the rise and fall of his chest.

"You'll never make it, Drake. You've got the whole town to ride through, and you'll never make it."

This was the showdown.

Drake mounted his black first, so as to keep himself between the crowd and Midge. He sat turned in the saddle with the shotgun across his lap while Midge and Etienne stepped up. Gerder's crowd began to spread out, moving in nervous little eddies toward the other curb. Jack Berry started to shift in the direction of Corral Street.

"Stop it," said Drake swiftly. "Stand right where you are! Gerder, if anybody starts firing on me, I'll shoot you. I swear I'll burn you down in cold blood, no matter who it is!"

But the others continued their spreading movement, and Gerder had begun backing toward the water trough in front of the livery barn next to his saloon. Drake realized it would be but a moment before the men at the fringes would

144

be out of his control. Etienne understood how he wanted it, and had begun moving Midge's dun forward at a slow, deliberate walk, but Drake knew it couldn't be like that now. He was about to speak when Midge shouted.

"Drake, watch out! Berry . . . !"

It took all the efforts in Drake not to turn toward Berry. "Jack," he shouted, "Gerder gets it if you . . . !" Then the shot cut him off, and his horse screamed shrilly, rearing up, and though Barton Gerder was still out there in the open, Drake couldn't bring himself to down the man in cold blood, and he twisted around in the saddle of the plunging horse for Berry.

There was a phaeton parked beyond the hitch rack almost at the corner of this side of the street, and Jack Berry had thrown himself behind that for his protection with his first shot. He fired again, and Drake's flat-topped Stetson was jerked from his head. All Drake could see of Berry were his legs through the spoked wheels of the phaeton, and he let go both barrels. Then he dropped the Greener, whirling to keep from being thrown off his horse without seeing the effect of his shot.

With the scattering crowd shouting and pulling their guns all about him, Drake screamed at Midge and Etienne: "Go on, I'm with you, go on . . . !"

He saw that Gerder had thrown himself behind the water trough, hauling out his gun, but as the man rose up, Etienne's LeMat roared, chipping bark off the hollow, undressed log of the trough, forcing Gerder to throw himself back to the ground. Drake slammed a fist into the neck of his screaming, rearing black, knocking it down, and then kicked it viciously in the belly. The horse jumped forward with the pain, stumbling before it got all four feet going. Drake questioned that, momentarily, but the horse was in full gallop now, and he was choking in the dust boiling up from the two horses ahead of him.

"Get their animals," shouted Gerder, jumping up from the water trough and opening fire, "get their animals . . . !"

But Drake was already past the bulk of the crowd, and a last man threw himself toward the curb from in front of the charging trio, too occupied with saving his own skin to use his gun. The shouts grew dim behind Drake, and he urged his black to catch up with Midge. They had passed the intersection of Convent and Ochoa where the horse stumbled again, and it came to Drake abruptly then. No wonder the animal had screamed and reared at Berry's first shot; it hadn't been merely spooked by the gunfire, it had been hit. Even with the realization, Drake felt the black stumble a third time beneath him, and sensed how it was and kicked free as the horse went to its knees. Had he gotten free a moment later, he would have been thrown over its head;

as it was, he rolled off to the side, with some control over his own precipitation, striking with his left foot first and taking most of the shock on the soft part of his buttocks, then going on down to tumble it off on his shoulders. He rolled into the high curb with a force that stunned him and heard his own groan from very far away as he tried to rise. The black lay out in the street with its forefeet twisted beneath it. The sidewalk above him clattered to someone's feet and he heard the man shout in a hoarse voice: "It's Drake, it's Laramie Drake!"

There was the creak of batwings, and the sidewalk groaned to the weight of more men, clattering as they moved over it. Drake got to his hands and knees, facing back toward Ochoa. Beyond the intersection, he could see a scattered bunch of riders coming, some of them just breaking away from the racks down in front of Gerder's Saloon and the other buildings near Corral. He caught at a rough pole supporting the wooden overhang above pulling himself erect, and the men near the curb shifted back on the sidewalk indecisively. Drake saw one man's hand move down, and then stop, and he shoved himself out toward the middle of the street, fumbling beneath his coat for the Reid.

"Go on!" he screamed hoarsely at Midge and Etienne, where they had hauled up their horses halfway down the block, and were turning. "Go on, Gerder's coming and you'll never make it if you come back. Do you hear me, Etienne! Go on, damn you, go on!"

He was faced around enough to see the first rider cross Ochoa, and it was Italy, with Barton Gerder right behind him, and they both had their guns out. The brass cylinder on the Knuckle Duster caught the sun in a brazen flash as Drake pulled it out, spreading his legs and shaking his head to clear the wool out. Then the ground was shaking beneath his feet, and he was almost knocked over by the sweaty flank of the big dun.

"Climb up!" shouted Midge, her red hair flying about her flushed face. "You didn't think we'd leave you? Climb up."

"Damn you," he said, but there was a wry smile lifting the corner of his mouth as he grabbed her leg and slipped his foot into the stirrup she had vacated. Facing toward the animal's rump, he pulled himself up behind the cantle, arms around her waist. Etienne had necked his sweating albino around them, beginning to fire at Gerder. Drake saw Italy haul his horse to a sudden hock-splitting halt, and then roll off the side into the street.

"Get him!" shouted Gerder, not even trying to pull his horse aside as it clattered over Italy, waving his gun at the men on the sidewalk. "Get Drake, I tell you . . . !"

The dun broke into a gallop under Midge's boot

heels, and then a dead run, and the frame houses of the residential district began to make a blurred pattern past them as they raced toward Congress. Drake turned them down this street toward the Santa Cruz River, breaking from the scattered adobe hovels on the outskirts of town into the first stand of black cottonwoods. In the marshy ground west of the river proper they turned north, slowing to a walk through the somber, stunted post oaks. They could hear Gerder's riders crashing through the cane and pussy willows behind. When Drake reached the spot he approximated to be opposite Alameda, he turned them westward again, reaching the solid ground with mud and gramma dropping off the horse's legs.

"Drake," said the girl sharply, "you're going right back into town."

"Which is the last place Gerder will look for us," he said.

V

A wild turkey was gobbling somewhere up in the higher timber and a chicken hawk was making lazy circles in the smoky sky above the crested ridges, and the three of them walked their horses down the narrow road that lowered itself like a white ribbon gently down the dark timbered slope into the flats below. It was two days after

Tucson. As Drake had said, Gerder wasn't looking for them to head directly back into town, and had probably spent an hour coursing the marshy ground west of the river, while they rode west on Alameda until they struck the Tanque Verde Road, reaching Drake's house in the mountains late that night. Dropping now into the Pinaleno Basin, Drake eased himself in the saddle with the stiffness of the long ride east from the Tanques Verdes, his voice irritable.

"It seems crazy to be carrying on any regular business while this thing about you is up in the air."

"What good would it do you to stay back at your spread?" asked Midge. "Besides, you already contracted to take this herd on. You can't afford to lose the money breaching the contract would mean. I've caused you enough trouble already."

He glanced at her from under his dark brow, trying to define the feeling in him. She was so unlike the other women he had known; the freshness of her, the purity, caught at him sometimes like this, when he could see the fruit-like curve of her young cheek beneath the tilt of her level hat brim, the lithe youth of her slim body in the square cut of the blue denim ducking suit. Then he saw Etienne, watching him from the other side of the girl.

"*Oui*, Drake," the fat Frenchman chuckled, "*oui. . . .*"

The laugh made the girl turn to Etienne. "What?" she said, and then she saw how he was looking past her to Drake and twisted the other way to the gambler. "What is it?"

"Nothing." Drake turned his eyes ahead, wondering if the sudden heat in his face meant he was flushing, and Etienne's chuckle angered him. The first haze raised by the cattle gathered in the basin had reached them now, and the road reached the bottom lands and left the flank of the Pinalenos, turning through a snake fence that crawled across the grassed flats. Now Drake could hear the bawl of cattle, and he felt an excitement fill him. *His* cattle. It pleased him to be able to say that. His cattle. He hadn't realized how much all this would mean to him. Waco Simms, Drake's ramrod, came riding out from the herd to meet them now, a lean, dusty man with dim origins in Texas he never referred to. Sitting his big double-rigged roping saddle with a slouchy ease, he raised a scarred, calloused hand to his hat brim for Midge, and turned keen gray eyes on Drake.

"Some old Mexican black horns in the bunch. They don't carry as much beef as the whitefaces, but they're good enough stock. Should take us the rest of this day to tally out the number you wanted. Delhaven was supposed to send out a crew to help us, but all he did was have one man to rep for him. Left us short-handed."

Drake saw the eager light in Midge's eyes. "I could help."

"Don't be silly, Midge," said Drake. "We haven't reached that point yet."

"But I want to do something, Drake," she said. "Waco, tell him I could help."

Waco scratched the lobe of his ear, grinning wryly. "I seen her work them Anchor cattle when I was repping for Hazard, Drake. She is right handy with a dally."

Drake started to say something, but saw the stubborn pout that had entered the girl's under lip and shrugged, smiling himself. Midge rode ahead with Waco back to where they were working the cattle, and Etienne sidled his albino in close to Drake's animal.

"So you don't know what to do with her?" The Frenchman chuckled.

Drake turned sharply. "What do you mean?"

"You make a better nursemaid than you realize," said Villeneu. "Or than you want to admit. Why don't you put in a petition for yourself as guardian of the girl?"

"Don't be obtuse, Villey."

"You're going to miss her when she goes, Drake. Already the house is a different place. You weren't even restless last night. You sat in your big chair and smoked your pipe and listened to her read like a complacent old man."

Drake gigged his horse ahead impatiently, angry

at himself for not being willing to admit Etienne was right, yet withdrawing from it somehow. She was only a kid. He was thirty-five years old, and she was only a kid, and it didn't make a hand that way.

They had about a hundred head left to brand, and Midge dismounted from her dun and began to unhitch the saddle. Drake stepped off near the branding fires where a tall, angular man in a flat-topped black hat was standing with a brand book. Waco introduced him as Davis Witmer, the man repping for Karl Delhaven, owner of the Kid-On-A-Rail cattle they were turning over to Drake. A rider hazed in a cow and dabbed his dally on and the ground shook beneath Drake as the animal went down. Another hand hog-tied her with peales before she could slip the dally.

"Hot iron!" he called, and a third man got a branding iron from the fire and came on the run. "Brindle heifer, swallow-fork, Kid-On-A-Rail."

"Brindle heifer, swallow-fork, Kid-On-A-Rail," repeated Witmer, writing it down in his book.

Drake watched them draw a line through the Kid-On-A-Rail brand with a bar stamp, and then use his own new Double Deuces stamping iron to burn on the pair of twos. The Kid-On-A-Rail earmark had been a swallow-fork, and the heifer bawled raucously when the cowhand grabbed her ear to cut Drake's seven undercut in. Then they jerked off the peales and let the animal scramble erect to be hazed into the herd that had already been worked over. It was then Drake saw that Midge had picked out a pinto pony from a bunch Waco had in the rope corral near the cottonwoods, and was saddling it up.

"Waco," he said sharply, "I didn't think she meant cutting."

"What else?" grinned Simms. "That kid should have been a boy, Drake. She'll be all right. Release one of my cutters for the fires, and we can work that much faster."

Midge trotted the pinto out, her hands light and deft on the reins feeling him out. As soon as she reached the herd, Drake began to realize how good she was. Cutting cattle was one of the most demanding jobs, requiring a singular skill and daring, and she went into it with the swift drive of an old hand, choosing a big steer near the flank of the bunch and cantering in on his quarter. The steer boogered and broke from the herd, giving her a line between the other animals and the single beef.

"That pinto's a good chopper," said Waco. "Real peg horse. He can turn on a biscuit and never cut the crust. Wouldn't trust him with many . . . there, see."

The pinto had given the appearance of getting too far ahead of the steer, on the inside, but when the beef turned to try and get back in the herd, the pony spun on a hind foot and was in between the steer and the herd so fast the beef's head jerked up in surprise, and it whirled around to run toward the fire again. Hazing the cow on in toward the fires, the pony worked over to the left side of its own accord, and Midge shook out her dally. Within ten feet of Drake she dabbed it on, the pinto squatting like a jack rabbit, and before the steer had hit, the two men branding had run in with their peales to hog-tie the animal and throw Midge's rope off. As she snaked it in and turned back to the herd, she threw a happy smile at Drake.

"*Sacre*, she actually enjoys it," said Etienne. "A man who was planning to build a spread would do well to hitch up with a woman like that. He could just sit back and let her do all the cow work."

"Long yearling, swallow-fork, Kid-On-A-Rail," Witmer was saying, writing it down in his book, and Waco had begun to squint up at the clouds sifting over the ridges of the Pinalenos to the east, muttering to himself: "Don't like them thunderheads. Spring rain'd turn this roundup into a bog ride."

Drake had heard them abstractedly. A man had ridden in through the snake fence on a big white horse that looked like livery, and he was walking it steadily toward the branding fires. He was thick-set and slope-shouldered, and must have been able to slip his choke collars on over his head.

"Well, Binder," said Drake. "How is P.R. doing?"

155

"See you alone?" said Albert Binder.

Drake shrugged, moved away from the fires, leaving Etienne with Waco. Binder followed on the mare till Drake halted, then got off with some effort. He took out a fresh cigar, offered it to Drake. Drake declined, and Binder bit off the end, spitting it out with a peculiar grimace.

"Nice job you did in Tucson other day," he said, as if he had been born with only so many words to use and intended to make them last to the end. "Didn't think any man could walk through that crowd the way you did. Gerder spent half the day hunting for you down river way. About blew his top when he heard you'd ridden back through town on Alameda pretty as you please. Now, Drake, I . . ."

"Represent the Pacific Railroad Corporation," said Drake. "I know. I'm sorry if I was rude the other day. I guess you understand now why I was in such a hurry. I hadn't realized things would be quite that tight when I hit town. Not me, so much. The girl. What about Pacific Railroad? You can have all afternoon, now, if you want."

"Know they've been building to Tucson from Bisbee. Going straight through the Tanques Verdes saves them several hundred miles of track. Gap's the only way through. How much you want for it?"

"If you're talking about Apache Gap, I don't own it."

Albert Binder looked as if he were regarding the most stupid man in the world. "Don't try to give us that, Drake. Might have hidden it from Tucson all this time, but we know everything. What's your price?"

Drake's irritation was rapidly becoming anger. "I don't own the Gap. What makes you think I do?"

"Investigators," said Binder. "What I am. Maybe you want me to open the bid. Say twenty thousand."

His words came out tinny and mechanical, and his eyes were hard and bright and opaque on Drake all the time, and Drake felt the scar pattern draw taut across his cheek with the bunching of his jaw. He tried to keep his voice under control.

"I don't see how your investigators could find out I own Apache Gap. The nearest private land to the Gap I know of is Hazard's Lazy Hook. His north pastures run up to Cochise Ridge, over-looking the Gap. Why don't you go to him?"

"Won't admit owning land that controls the Gap?" said Binder.

"I won't admit owning anything I don't own."

Binder took out his cigar again but didn't look at it. "What kind of a game, Drake?"

"I might ask you the same thing," said Drake heatedly.

"Bucking an organization's busted bigger men than you, Drake." The staccato intonation to his words gave them a strange menace.

Drake leaned forward till his face almost met Binder's. "I don't know what the hell this is about, but I'd advise you not to threaten me."

Binder hadn't moved back. "Not threatening. Don't have to. You're intelligent enough to see implications. Can understand what might happen if you don't play ball. P.R. wants the Gap. Get it from you, one way, the other. Which way you want?"

Drake's answer was stopped by the clap of thunder; he straightened, realizing only now how dark the sky had become. The first drops of rain touched his face. The thunder came again, in deafening waves of sound, and he could see how the cattle were beginning to bawl and plunge in a frenzy. Waco Simms had mounted the men at the fires and ran them in to help the circle riders start milling the cattle so they wouldn't stampede. One of the cutters who had been within the smaller herd forced his way to the fringes and broke free as the cattle began running more wildly in their mill. The thunder died momentarily, and Drake could hear the shouts of the men and the crazed bawl of cows, the dust rising up beneath the whirling vortex of beef only to be beaten back again by the slanting rain. Then, over all the other sounds, it came to Drake.

"Midge, get out of the herd!" he yelled. Then to Waco: "Why the hell didn't you tell me she was still cutting inside? Get her out, damn you, get her out . . . !"

It was a sudden fear that swept Drake then, for he could see the small shadowy figure in the center of the smaller herd that had not yet been marked with Drake's Double Deuces, bobbing and jerking in a mad effort to get free. With the sweep of his arm, Drake shoved Binder aside and broke into a headlong run, the rain pelting at his hat brim in rhythm to the pound of his boots. The circle riders were throwing their horses at the cattle in an effort to break the mill, but the steers made a solid wall of hurtling, whirling beef, and already one man had been thrown back, unhorsed. Then it was Waco's voice again, even as Drake saw it happen, dimly there, within the herd.

"I didn't know she was in there. Why the hell didn't you tell me? Break that mill, you fools, break that mill. Oh, my God, she's down, she's down!"

As a boy, Drake had seen a top hand do it in the middle of a spring-swollen river. The cattle had been in a mill there, too, and the hand had broken the mill that way, reaching the center and hooking onto an old lead steer and driving it right through the circling beefs to the opposite bank. This wasn't in the water, and he knew there would be no lead steer to help him. But he did not consider failure; there was no time for that. He only saw how the men had failed in breaking the mill from the outside, and he remembered how that top hand had done it in the river, and he meant to try it the same way.

"Drake," screamed Waco, "don't be a damn fool! You can't get in there that way . . . !"

But Drake had already reached the fringe, quartering in until he was running in the same direction as the frenzied, circling, bawling cattle. It was all a blanket of sodden dust and pelting rain and running, blabbering beeves after that, and the steers were so full of primordial fear of the storm that they paid no heed to him as he threw himself into it. Drake missed his hold the first time and stumbled and almost fell and threw himself at the next running cow to come into his vision, and missed that time, too, and went down then, bowled over by the animal's flank. Chest heaving, mouth working with the pain in him, he struggled to his feet, dodging a heifer that came clattering around the fringe of the mill, and then he saw the longhorn passing him, and reached out for his hold on that.

"Drake, you damn fool, you damn fool . . . !"

But Drake had finally made his mount, running along beside the steer and grabbing the horn and leaping up like an Indian. Stunned and battered, coat ripped by the horns, he rode the steer around the mill. They were so tightly packed his inside leg was continually bumped and mashed by the bodies of the steers. He saw a big brockle-faced steer stumble and go down, to be trampled beneath the hoofs of those behind, the gap it left filled immediately. Then Drake was rising up to do it. There were only some fifty-odd left in this herd, and, crouched like that to leap, Drake could see the center of the mill.

The cowhands always started the mill from the outside, turning the head of the running bunch till the leaders met the tail and the herd was going in a circle that gradually closed on itself and stopped when the cattle became too tightly packed to run any more. The outer circles were already pressing in so close they formed a solid mass of withers and rumps beneath Drake, but the inner ranks were still loose, with the open space yet showing in the very center. And in that space, Drake saw the peg-horse's head, appearing now and then amid the flashing horns and rising hump ribs of the cows. He knew a moment's prayer that the cutting horse was as smart as it had looked working the cows, and then he made his leap.

A slashing horn caught at his pants, and he heard the cloth rip, and felt the stabbing pain as the sharp tip raked his leg, and he threw himself on forward, desperately seeking footing on the tightly packed backs, clawing at the horns to hold himself from falling. And all the time he was thinking of that horse. Stand still. Don't break now. For God's sake, just stand still. It's the only chance.

His foot slipped between two steers and he went to his crotch in the fetid press of bodies. The pain nauseated him, and his leg was crushed between the running animals. With bleeding hands he caught at another horn, hauling himself up on the steer's back, sprawled across the animal. Blindly he fought to crouch and leap again, his actions more instinctive than conscious now, and he must have been talking like that a long time before he heard himself.

"Just stand still. Good little horse. Damned good little horse. It's her only chance. Stay right there. Good little chopping horse. Oh, damn you, stay there, stand still, stay there . . ."

Then he realized it was his voice that had made the horse whirl. He was that close. It seemed as if he had been riding those steers for an eternity, yet it must have been but a few seconds from the first jump. With a last wild cry, he leaped from the steer, hurtling bodily over the inside rank and striking the horse with a stunning force. He felt the mount stagger under the blow, and brace itself, and reel back against him. He had caught at the saddle leather, and he came out of the haze like that, fallen against the pinto with the inner ranks of steers bumping up against him now, pressed in by the outer animals. He realized there was but another instant. Midge lay between the pinto's forelegs, her face bloody, her clothes ripped.

"Hold it, hold it," Drake gasped at the horse, letting go the stirrup leather to reach for her, "good little horse, just stand, just hold it." His greatest fear in that moment was that the animal would break and bolt in this last instant. He caught Midge by the shoulders and pulled her free. Her body was light and soft and limp in his arms, the sodden red hair brushing his face as he heaved her across the pony's withers, then he swung aboard the animal himself, leg striking a steer, and pulled his Knuckle Duster. The pinto was staggering back and forth as the cows struck it from all sides now, and Drake could feel it quivering with fear beneath him, yet it waited his command. He kicked the horse at the same time he fired, and the mount leaped forward as the big steer stumbled and fell, leaving a gap for that moment in the running ranks.

The .41 Reid packed a big punch, but it was only his nearness to the cattle that enabled him to down them instantly like that, picking a spot behind their ears. He was practically riding on top of them, and he rammed sideways into a big sorrel steer and almost touched its head with the tip of his Knuckle Duster when he fired; the steer jerked perceptibly, went to its knees, then disappeared beneath the trampling hoofs, and Drake had rammed the pony into the gap, firing again, again, again.

Behind him there was no open space left in the center, where Midge had lain the moment before, and Drake could see how the steers of the inner ranks were constantly being sucked into that whirlpool forming the hub of the mill, eventually to go down and be trampled beneath the vortex of running, smashing animals. Then Drake pulled the trigger on his Reid, and it didn't buck in his hand, and he knew that was all. He was too exhausted, too beaten for feeling much at that, and with a hopeless sob he slumped forward over Midge, dripping rainwater off his soggy hair and blood off his face onto her torn blue denims, letting the pinto have its head to move helplessly around the mill with the bawling cattle. A steer's horn hooked him in the side, and he did not even cry out with the pain. His legs were pinned to the pinto's lathered sides by pressure of the hot, stinking, hairy bodies.

Finally, it came to him, through the apathy of pain and exhaustion, that the steers were not whirling as fast as before. The mill had wound up so tight it wouldn't whirl any more, and the cattle were slowing. From the fringes, men called softly now, working gently at the cattle, cutting off one at a time so as not to frighten them again. When Drake saw his chance, he broke through the last few between him and the open; he could drive the pinto no farther than the edge, and slid off the horse, almost going to his knees. Waco Simms and Villeneu were beside him, and he heard himself mumbling brokenly.

"Horse was in there standing over her, standing right over her . . ."

"What'd I tell you," said Simms softly. "Best peg horse in Arizona. Smartest chopper you kin find."

"Small herd, see," sobbed Drake. "Couldn't have done it with a big bunch. Too far to the middle. Lucky it was a small herd, see. Started going down in the middle right after I got out. That's what she would've gotten. That horse stood right there. Didn't move an inch. Small herd, see."

"We know, *mon ami*, we know," said Villeneu, as if he were speaking to a child, and tried to draw Drake away. "You've taken a bad beating, *hein*? You better lie down."

"No." Drake pulled away from him. "No. Midge, Midge?"

"She looks all right," said Waco. They had laid her down in the grass, and he was dabbing at the cut on her forehead while a cowhand went for some water. "A horn must have hooked in her clothes here and pulled her off the pony and she struck her forehead when she hit."

She was opening her eyes even then, and she looked up past Simms, and saw him, and said it softly: "Drake."

"Midge," he said, and that was all he had waited for, and he felt himself sagging back into Etienne's fat arms, and all the pain and exhaustion receded from him with the swift wash of a wave leaving the shore, and his consciousness left the same way.

VI

The Tanques Verdes eastward from Apache Gap were rich with springs and the barrel cactus marched across the flatlands, bearing its yellow wreath of delicately fluted flowers proudly, and higher up the slopes the tree toads filled the night with their endless chirping. From where he hunkered on a bare ridge top, Drake could see the fires of the cow camp below him; straight ahead he could see where this slope melted into Apache Gap itself, a narrow notch through the Verdes that cattlemen had been using to reach the spreads beyond since the first Spanish black horns had been driven into Tucson.

Drake had taken his Winchester from the saddle boot, and when he realized the tree toads had stopped their chirping, his hand tightened about the carbine and he let himself slide down behind the rock. It came again, the sibilance of some movement through the gramma in the timber below him. Then the moon shone on the figure moving out into the park. Drake rose slightly to show himself. The figure halted momentarily.

"Drake?"

"Yes," he said softly.

Midge moved on toward him across the open meadow, reaching the uplift of sandstone con-

166

cealing him. "I saw you leave. You aren't well enough to go wandering around at night like this. You took a terrible beating from those cattle day before yesterday, and this long ride hasn't helped any."

"I want to get them to the Double Deuces as quick as possible," he said. "Waco saw a rider up here near sunset."

She dropped down beside him abruptly. "Gerder?"

"I don't think Gerder would know of this drive," he said. "There was that man representing the P.R., Albert Binder. He left before I could speak with him again after that mill."

"But why should he . . . ?"

"I don't know." He waved his hand impatiently.

Her laugh was small and soft. "You're not like any gambler I ever saw, Drake."

"If you mean I don't have a dead pan, I can't help that," he said. "I always did well enough without it."

"More than that. Most of the card men I've known were jaded, world-weary." She touched his face, hesitantly. "Where did you get those scars?"

"A man got after me with a broken bottle in Abilene."

She lifted her head to look at him, and a decision came into her face slowly.

"Drake, were you in love with Donna?"

Was that what she had been leading up to? "Why do you ask?"

She lowered her eyes suddenly, and in the moonlight he could see the delicate flush tinting her cheeks. "The way she looked at you, the way she spoke . . ."

He had the sudden sense of holding something infinitely fragile, that even the wrong breath might shatter, and his voice was sober when it came: "No, Midge, I wasn't in love with Donna."

There was an ineffable relief in the way Midge took her breath, without looking up at him, and watching the soft glow of moonlight across her red hair, he realized how much it pleased him to sit out here beside her, with the tree toads making their music and the heady fragrance of the spring grasses lifting up to them. Then he caught himself. *Damned fool,* he thought, *with a kid like this.* He forced himself to speak of something that took him away from it.

"Midge, did it ever occur to you what would happen to the cattlemen in the Tanques Verdes if the Río Caballo was diverted at this eastern end of Apache Gap?"

She glanced at him, wondering, perhaps, why he had changed the subject so abruptly. "Río Caballo runs right through the Gap. Cut it off at this end, and you'd deprive most of the Tanques Verdes spreads of their water supply."

"And that's just what the Pacific Railroad will

do, if it takes the Gap through. There's a lot of places in the Gap that aren't wide enough for the Río Caballo and the P.R. tracks, too. The river would have to be diverted from this end, since its source is east of the Gap."

He heard her indrawn breath. "Drake, do you think that's what Gerder was talking about when he stopped me? He said something about the Gap."

"I'm beginning to think that's what this whole thing is about," said Drake. "Farrow's murder, maybe even your father's murder. Everybody knew the P.R. was building from Bisbee, but we took it for granted, coming from the south as they were, that they'd head around the southwest tip of the Tanques Verdes and avoid going through the mountains. It seems their engineers figured out a shorter route by cutting down on the eastern side and taking Apache Gap through. Who owns that strip on Cochise Ridge just above the Gap?"

"Dad used to," said Midge. "But he sold those pastures to Eben Hazard years ago."

"That's what I thought," said Drake. "Gerder must know it, too. Then why should he be hounding you in connection with it? And why should P.R. think I own land controlling the Gap?"

Midge sounded startled. "You?"

"It looks," he said, "as if they were just about as confused as we are." Then he stopped, because the tree toads had ceased chirping down in the timber again, and Midge had heard it, too, and had lived in this country long enough to know what that meant.

She slid down the uplift beside him till they lay, two shadowy forms barely perceptible against the rugged contour of the sandstone. One side of her body was warm against him, and he could feel the regular rise and fall of her breathing, and it told him something of the girl, that she could lay there and wait for this so calmly. He knew his own breathing was accelerated, and he kept searching the trees fringing the park. A small wind came up, growing through the timber below. Then it was the man, moving out of the pines in a deliberate direction, casting a glance over his shoulder as if to get a last look at something, and the moonlight revealed who he was, as it had revealed Midge.

"Having a look at my cows, Colorado?" said Drake.

Colorado Carnes turned slowly, not trying to raise the Springfield he held in his hand, as if, from long experience, he knew whoever spoke from cover like that would have a gun on him already. He was a tall, lean man, and Drake remembered when his well-tailored suit had been cleaner. He had his gray trousers tucked into fancy-stamped spurless Justins, and his flat-topped hat slanted at a cocky angle across his long-jawed face, hiding it in black shadow.

"Come on in and don't try to use the lead-pusher. It's Drake."

"Laramie," said Colorado, and moved forward openly. "You hooked up with that herd in the gully?"

"Driving them," said Drake. "You look like you've been sleeping in a ditch all week. Hiding out?"

"My connections with Face Card aren't any healthier than yours," said Colorado. "Being his bodyguard was dangerous enough when he was alive. With him dead, it's like I'd been holding a loaded gun to my head all this time and suddenly decided to cock it."

"Is it?"

Colorado stopped in front of the uplift abruptly, and the heartiness was gone from his voice. "You sound skeptical."

"Was that the only reason you left Tucson in such a hurry you forgot to collect the two weeks' pay owed you?" said Drake, and rose with his Winchester cuddled in one elbow so that it still pointed in Colorado Carne's general direction.

Colorado seemed to sense what was inside Drake, and his mouth broke into a loose-lipped grin. "What else?"

"Who murdered Face Card?"

Midge had stood, then, and Colorado's grin broadened without gaining any mirth. "Ah, the

Lawrence kid. I heard you had appointed yourself her guardian, Drake. You're really up a crick, aren't you? Half the men in Tucson are after your hide because you were affiliated with Face Card Farrow, and the other half are looking to notch their guns with your gizzard because you took in Midge Lawrence."

Drake's voice was sharp. "You seem to know a lot for a man who took to the tules."

"I keep in touch," said Colorado. He leaned back slightly, shoving his hat back on his head so the light caught meagerly in his pale eyes. "I've been meaning to contact you anyway, Drake. I guess this is just luck, isn't it? As I say, I keep in touch. I know quite a bit about this business. Albert Binder, for instance." He laughed flatly as he saw what that had done to Drake. "Surprised? I told you I know quite a bit. Maybe some of it would interest you, Drake. Why, for instance, do you figure Pacific Railroad has pegged you as the owner of Apache Gap? You know you don't own it. I know. But P.R. thinks you do."

Drake moved through a cut in the uplift toward Colorado, tightening his grip on the Winchester involuntarily. "How do you know I don't own the Gap? Because you know who does own it?"

"Maybe." Colorado's slack-lipped grin irritated Drake, as it had always done. "Maybe I know a lot of things you'd like to know, Drake. It puts you in quite a spot, doesn't it, having P.R. figure you own the Gap and won't sell it to them. You saw Binder, you know what kind he is. He's got all the power of a big corporation behind him when he moves, and the methods he might use to get what he thinks you own wouldn't be nice. They could even reach the point of endangering your life, Drake. And whatever affects you, now affects Midge. That would put her between the frying pan and the fire, wouldn't it? Gerder coming at you from one side and Binder from the other."

"Colorado . . ." Drake had been goaded so long by evasions and mysteries that he forgot his rifle, unable to listen to Colorado any longer, dropping the Winchester and shouting as he leaped, all the bitter frustration of the past days erupting in him. "What do you know? Is this all mixed in together? Is Gerder after Midge for the same thing? Tell me, by God, or I'll kill you right here."

Perhaps Colorado hadn't realized how near Drake was to this, for he didn't even get his gun up before Drake struck him, and he had gone backward with the gambler's hands on his throat, sliding down between Drake's legs till Drake stood bent over, straddling him, shaking him.

"Drake . . ." Colorado tried for an instant to jam his rifle upward, but released it in a spasm of agony to claw at Drake's hands on his throat, choking the words out. "Drake, stop it. Kill me and you're killing the girl!"

"Killing the girl?" Drake hardly recognized his own voice, but it was what made him quit. He stood, spraddle-legged, above the man, his hands still on Colorado's scrawny neck, panting heavily. Colorado tried to get back his breath with a sick, hollow sound, his face contorted, and finally managed to force that slack-lipped smile again.

"Yeah," he breathed hoarsely. "I thought so. I thought maybe it was that way. You think some of Midge? I don't blame you. She's a nice little package . . ."

Drake was shaking him again, voice savage. "Shut up. Tell me what you meant about killing her."

Colorado licked his lips, before saying: "Let me up."

"No, tell me."

"Let me up or you don't get a crumb!"

Drake was trembling with his effort at control; he twisted around so he could see Midge. She had kicked away Carne's Springfield and was holding the Winchester tightly, and sight of her standing so tensely there, her face set, backing him up, made Drake draw his hands off Colorado's neck and step back. The lean man rolled over to an elbow, then rose, brushing at his clothes, one hand holding his neck.

"You always did have strong fingers," he muttered sullenly. He tilted his head down to look at Drake from under his brows, and

174

something sly came into his fuliginous eyes. "I shouldn't tell you anything after that."

"Colorado."

"Never mind." Colorado held up a defensive hand as Drake bent forward. "You'll get it, but you'll pay for it, believe me. That little business will cost you extra. Like I said, if anything happens to me, that's just as good as killing Midge. I'm the only one who can tell you what they're after, Drake, and where it is."

"What who's after?" Drake's voice held a desperation.

"Gerder," said Colorado. "The P.R. Maybe even more have guessed about it now . . . Hazard or Judge Petrie, or any one of a dozen who've been mixed up with Face Card and the rest of Tucson's dirty politics. Gerder wanted it bad enough to try and kill you in your own house to get Midge. You can drive Albert Binder to the same extremes, or worse, if he keeps thinking money won't buy the Gap from you. You know as well as I do what will eventually happen if you can't stop them, Drake. You can't buck them all forever . . . you're one against a dozen, and it'll be more all the time. Sooner or later one of them will get you. It doesn't matter whether it's Gerder or Binder or Hazard. It doesn't matter who it is. And then what will happen to Midge?" He took a hasty step backward at the savage look that crossed Drake's face. "I'm just telling you, Drake. You wanted it. I'm telling you. You know it yourself. That's the way it'll be, sooner or later, unless you can stop them."

"And you possess what it takes?"

"Not personally," said Colorado. "But maybe I can get my hands on it."

"On what?"

"On what they're all after."

"The Gap?"

Colorado's grin was condescending. "You see what a helpless position you're in, Drake. No, not exactly the Gap."

"Then Gerder's after something different than Binder."

"Is he?" said Colorado.

"Binder's after the Gap?"

"I didn't say he wasn't," said Colorado. "All I'm saying is what I can get my hands on isn't exactly the Gap, but it's what they're after."

"How will it stop them trying to get Midge?"

Colorado raised his blond brows. "Aren't you interested in yourself?"

"How will it stop them trying to get her?"

Colorado shrugged. "You'll find that out when you get it."

Drake was filled with a frustrated confusion, and he had to hold himself from going for Colorado again. "I suppose there's a consideration."

"Ten thousand dollars might help."

"You dirty liar"—Drake had him by the throat again—"you damned dirty liar. You don't have

176

anything. Why should you take ten thousand from me when Binder's willing to lay twenty thousand across the board?"

"Drake, I told you," choked Colorado. "Take your hands off me or you won't get anything and you'll be just the same as putting a gun to Midge's head yourself." He almost fell when Drake released him, stumbling backward. He stood there, trying to get his breath again, and this time he didn't grin. "Okay. It's fifteen thousand now. For that, it's fifteen thousand." He saw the suspicion in Drake's smoldering black eyes and waved his thin hand. "Maybe I can't deal with Binder the way you can. Ever think of that? Why do you think he came to you in the first place? Do you think I wouldn't have sold it to him if I could?"

Drake's fists were opening and closing spasmodically. "What's the layout?"

"You know that old trapper's shack on Cochise Ridge above the Gap?" Drake shook his head, and Colorado turned momentarily to Midge. "You do, don't you, kid? Sure. Almost on the border of that strip your dad used to own on the other side of the ridge. I'll be there three days from now at dawn. That'll give you a chance to travel at night so nobody can spot you. Get it? Dawn, Tuesday next. You and Midge and fifteen thousand. Nothing else, nobody else. Try to pull a card from beneath your deck and you'll only be hurting Midge."

"How do I know I can trust you?"

"Either take that chance, or . . ." He turned his hand palm up, gesturing significantly enough toward Midge, and shrugging. Then the slack-lipped grin came again. "Is it a deal?"

Drake's voice was flat. "It is. But if you're lying to me, Colorado, I'll kill you."

The utter simplicity of the statement might have been what gave it such a deadliness, or the look in Drake's eyes. Colorado Carnes stopped grinning. He looked at Drake a moment, and his face had an odd, pale light. He took a breath.

"Okay," he said, still held by Drake's gaze. Then he turned to get his rifle. "Okay. Tuesday next. With fifteen thousand."

Midge stepped aside from where he had thrown the Springfield, still holding the Winchester on him. Bending to get his rifle, he looked up at her and attempted a smile, but it wouldn't seem to come, and in a sudden impatient way he picked up the bolt-action rifle, cast a last, furtive glance at Drake, then turned to swing off across the meadow in a long stiff stride.

"I wonder if I've made a mistake," muttered Drake, watching him go.

"I think Face Card Farrow was the one who made the mistake," said Midge soberly.

His dark head turned down to her. "What do you mean?"

"He should have chosen you, instead of Colorado Carnes, for his bodyguard," she said.

VII

The red flames crackled softly in the big rock fireplace of the Double Deuces house, and Etienne came through the kitchen door proudly bearing aloft a shining tureen, his chef's hat standing starched on his fat head and the sweat dribbling down the creases in his plump cheeks formed by a very satisfied smile.

"A special dinner to celebrate our safe arrival at the home spread with the cattle," he beamed. "*Coulis de Lapereau au Currie*. It is different from *Filets de Levraut a la Mornay* in that with *Coulis de Lepereau* the legs of the hare are used, *compre*, and in *Levraut a la Mornay* it is the loins and tenderloins. This is a much more complicated procedure, however. I spent twenty minutes rubbing the coulis through a sieve. In filets of hare *Mornay* there is none of that. Just take the filets of two young hares . . ."

"Set it down, will you, before it gets cold." Drake smiled.

The tureen made an offended thud on the ponderous oak table, and Etienne pouted. "*Mon ami*, you never let me finish telling how I cook *Filets de Levraut a la Mornay*. You wouldn't even let me finish telling *M'sieu* Pacific Railroads in the Coronado House the other day. I had just gotten to where I color the croutons with butter when you walked out on the porch with that shotgun and I had to follow. He seemed so interested, too."

"Shall I serve while you tell us how to cook filets of rabbits?" Midge laughed.

"Hare, hare," muttered Etienne peevishly, "not rabbit, *sacre bleu*," and waddled into the kitchen for *rice a l'Indienne* to garnish the coulis.

Midge went on talking as she served, telling Drake something about Waco and the herds. It was odd, Drake reflected, how Midge seemed to be the one who kept the conversation going, leading them into jokes without their realizing it till they were laughing. Perhaps she sensed Drake didn't want to discuss Gerder or Hazard or Colorado— she seemed to sense so many of his moods—or perhaps she realized any talk of that would have depressed them and ruined what Etienne had intended should be a gay supper party. And surprisingly enough, before they had finished with the entrée, Drake had forgotten Colorado and the rest. He had already sent Simms into Tucson with a draft on the bank for the $15,000, which halved his balance, and all during this Sunday he had been pondering the day after tomorrow, when they should meet Colorado; but now, under Midge's gay banter, it had left him momentarily. He found himself watching the way she tilted her head to one side when she was listening to

Etienne tell of Paris, and found himself liking it, and the infinite variation of expression in her eyes that came when she was talking, and the strange little half smile that caught at her lips when she realized he was watching her.

Etienne had found something to do in the kitchen after supper that left them alone in the living room, but he must have heard Midge retire about 11:00, for a few minutes later the kitchen door creaked open. Drake was sitting in the big Spanish armchair before the fire, pleasantly drowsy.

"She read to you some more," said Etienne.

Drake glanced at the book, still open on the bear rug of the hearth. "She finds it strange for a gambler to enjoy Browning."

"She finds many things strange about you, as others before her have, *mon ami*," said Etienne. "She finds it strange that you didn't kill Hazard when he provoked you to."

Drake knocked dottle from his cold pipe, shrugging. "She'd just been listening to her father or someone."

Etienne smiled. "She also finds it strange that you haven't got a dead pan, and don't constantly play with a deck of cards, and don't affect the expected bored cynicism."

"Don't, Villy, will you?" Drake shook his head from side to side.

"Why not? Are you afraid to discuss how she

feels about you?" Etienne bent to pick up the book. "She finds it strange that you enjoy Browning, yet she seems to enjoy him, too. She seems to enjoy a lot of things you do. It has been pleasant, having her here, Drake. Will you be as sorry when this mess is over and she goes as I will be? It's almost been worth fighting all of Tucson to have her around."

"Don't be a fool." Drake's voice was impatient despite himself. "I'll find her a *proper* guardian as soon as she's out of danger. We can't keep her here like this any longer than is necessary."

"Why not, Drake?" Etienne was serious now. "Why not keep her here always? Don't you know how she feels about you?"

Drake got out of the chair, pacing restlessly toward the end of the room. "I said don't be a fool. I've just helped her. Naturally she feels some gratitude."

"Not gratitude, Drake. You know what it is. You've seen it. You just don't want to admit it to yourself."

Drake whirled on him, jerking his hand in that frustrated way. "She's just a kid. How does she know how she feels?"

"She's a woman, Drake. Could a kid have gone through all this hell the way she has? *Non.* You just keep trying to tell yourself she's a kid because you're afraid to lower that barrier between the two of you. I've seen the way you watch her, Drake. You never watched Donna that way."

"But I'm thirty-five, and she's only nineteen." Drake stopped, realizing that in itself was an admission of his feelings, and he saw how Etienne was smiling.

"Don't try to tell me you are that conventional, Drake." The Frenchman giggled. "Wasn't it the Brownings who had ten years' difference in their ages? How can you possibly read his works? I'm surprised he wasn't excommunicated."

"Oh, stop it, stop it. . . ."

Drake turned to the fire, hearing Etienne put the book away in the case at one end of the stone fireplace. He felt like a fool, but he knew Etienne had taken no offense, and when the Frenchman spoke again, it was cheerful enough.

"You've been looking over those papers of Farrow's, *hein*? Found anything?"

"Nothing I can really use," said Drake dispiritedly. "There is part of a letter that might help against Hazard. It's from Gerder to Hazard. I don't know how Farrow got hold of it. He had a genius for that sort of thing. No date on the letter, but in it Gerder says his mouth is shut about the Corral Street fire as long as Hazard doesn't try to squeeze him out of his spread."

"*Oui*," said Etienne. "Gerder picked up his Pothook spread about that time. A couple of months after the fire, wasn't it? I remember we all wondered why Hazard allowed Gerder to do it. The Pothook gave Gerder access to those sinks on Hazard's southern pastures, and Hazard had never let any other man use his water before. But what could Gerder know about the Corral Street fire that would give him a hold over Hazard?"

"Who was burned out in the fire?" said Drake. "Eddie Neiman's general store was gutted. The old Maxeter Grain and Feed Barns."

"Maxeter could have been the one blocking Hazard's appointment to the chairmanship of the Tucson Cattlemen's Association," Etienne muttered. "Remember how hard Hazard was fighting to get the appointment. And Maxeter rode a big saddle in the T.C.A."

"And right after the fire, Maxeter resigned from the T.C.A.," said Drake. "He said the fire had ruined him."

"And Hazard is now chairman." Etienne grinned, then he shrugged. "But all this is mere supposition, Drake. You can't prove anything by that letter. Maybe Gerder *could* prove the fire was Hazard's doing, but you can't."

"I'll use it somehow . . . ," began Drake, but someone was running across the flagstones of the porch, and he made a half move toward his Knuckle Duster as the door was flung open. Waco Simms burst in, his lean face flushed from running.

"Hazard," he panted. "Big bunch coming up the

road. Already at the fence. Hazard and Gerder. They mean business, Drake."

Drake had already whirled to get the Winchester down from the mantel, slipping it out of its scabbard and dropping the leather case, scooping off a cardboard box of .30-30s. "Get Midge dressed, Etienne. Don't let her outside. Come on, Waco."

Waco Simms followed Drake onto the porch, closing the door behind them so the light wouldn't silhouette them to form targets. Drake could already feel the ground trembling faintly to the beat of many horses as he stepped onto the flagstones set into the earth, flush with the level of the surrounding compound. A support of the *portales* drew its dark line from the flagstones to the overhang above, forming a frame for the dark mass of riders as they poured around the end of the spur ridge that hid the fence from here and came on down the white ribbon of the roadway beneath the moonlight. One rider was ahead, his gun cracking out above the sound of hoofs. He hauled his lathered mount up at the edge of the porch, and throwing himself off with one hand gripping his shoulder, stumbled toward Drake.

"They got Andy!" he said. "We tried to hold them at the fence, but they got Andy."

"Get inside with that shoulder," said Drake, and then stepped from beneath the *portales* so the moonlight caught his white shirt brightly. He made a tall, broad-shouldered figure there, his legs straight and long beneath him, the Winchester drawing its significant line slantwise across the front of his flat belly. They saw him, and there was a perceptible diminution of their speed, and then the first man drew his horse to a halt, and the others slowed down of their own momentum as they passed him, halting one by one as they spread beyond him across in front of the house. Drake could see how big the mare was, as it pulled away from the others, before he recognized the man.

"Little different than going through a fence, I guess," said Waco Simms bitterly, and Drake knew he was thinking of the boy named Andy.

"Drake?" said the man on the big Appaloosa mare.

"You know it is, Hazard," said Drake.

"We came for the girl."

"Listen, Hazard." Something hoarse had entered Drake's voice. "She hasn't got it. Whatever you're after, she hasn't got it."

"Whatever I'm after?" Hazard's Appaloosa shifted restlessly. "All I'm after is Midge. She's my ward, and I'm not having her out here in any damned gambler's house like this."

"Don't deal me those deuces," said Drake. "You aren't after her because she's your ward. You don't care about that, you never did. Gerder's with you? You're after the same thing he is."

It was Gerder, then, gigging his dappled gelding in beside Hazard, taller than the other man, smaller about the waist. "You'd better hand her over, Drake. We aren't going away without her this time. We've got the law with us now, and whatever we do is legal."

"George?" said Drake.

It was a long moment before Sheriff George Kennedy reluctantly answered, unwilling to move his horse out of the line behind Hazard and Gerder. "Yeah, Drake. He's right. Please don't cause us any trouble. I got a warrant here for you for Midge's abduction."

"Who swore it out?"

Again the answer was late in coming. "Petrie."

The bitterness inside him entered Drake's voice now. "I'm glad all my friends are in on this. I'm glad you didn't leave any of them out, George. Good for you. I won't forget this, George. No matter what happens, I won't forget it."

"Drake, please. . . ."

"You don't care what they're after, do you, George? You know as well as I do Hazard isn't after Midge because she's his ward. You know that, don't you?" But Drake saw how it was now, with that many of them out there, and under his breath he spoke to Waco Simms. "Get Midge out the back and into that timber north of the house. I'll hold them here till you're free. It's the best we can do now." Then he raised his voice again. "I'm not handing her over, George. You hear that? Hazard? I'm not handing her over. You'll pay higher stakes for this than you ever did at my poker games. Hurry up, Waco, they're starting to spread. Hurry before they get around back. Waco, damn you. . . ."

Simms had been reluctant to leave Drake alone there, but finally he slipped through the door. Gerder must have seen the momentary spread of light behind Drake, for his voice came hard across the space between them.

"They're doing something. Get your men around the house, Hazard, they're doing something in there."

It was Drake's last effort to stop them, and his voice was strained. "All right, Hazard, you forced it. You've got your boots in the mud too deep to pull them out now. Can you hear me, Hazard? Maybe you didn't know what I got in town the other day. Gerder knows. Or maybe you came after that, too. Well, you won't get it, Hazard. Face Card Farrow's papers are in the hands of the marshal at Prescott right now, in a sealed envelope to be opened on my death. Do you hear me?"

They had heard him. He hadn't expected such a reaction. The movement out there stopped. A horse shifted, snorting restlessly, and for a moment that was the only sound. Then Hazard called to Drake and it sounded forced.

"What have Face Card's papers got to do with this?"

Drake felt the first flush of hope. "You know

what they've got to do with it. There's a lot of people in Tucson would like to know who was responsible for the Street fire, Hazard."

"What's that?" said Hazard. "Drake, you're crazy. . . ."

"Am I? Face Card Farrow had a number of interesting documents among his papers, Hazard. Make them public and half the men in Tucson would have to leave the country. Even a few honest, law-abiding citizens. Maybe the T.C.A. would be interested in finding the measures their present chairman took to get his appointment."

"You're bluffing." There was something shrill in Hazard's tone.

"Am I? Go ahead with this, then, and find out. Go ahead, Hazard. You're dealing now. You can put any cards you want in your hand."

He could see Hazard turn sharply to Gerder, and they had begun arguing. Hazard waved his arm, saying something to Gerder. Gerder shifted angrily in his saddle, answering. Hazard turned to look at the house once more, then jerked his head in a sharp, mandatory way, wheeling his Appaloosa savagely and spurring it into a sharp canter down the road. Half a dozen riders broke from the line behind to follow him, and Drake knew they would be the Lazy Hook crew. A last man turned his horse to follow Hazard.

"George," said Gerder loudly enough for Drake to hear.

Sheriff Kennedy hesitated, then stopped his horse, sitting there in a sullen slouch. Besides the sheriff, there were seven or eight men left that Drake could see. Gerder said something that started them spreading. A pair of them dismounted, hitching their horses in the cottonwoods across the road and moving at an angle that would take them to the side of the house.

"Gerder," shouted Drake in a final desperation, "haven't you got any feeling for the kid at all? She's just as liable to get hurt as any of us. Start shooting and you can't tell who you're liable to hit. Killing her won't get what you want. . . ."

The first shot cut him off, the slug singing lengthwise down the porch. The heavy *portale* would provide no protection from this angle, and he whirled toward one end, snapping a shot at the dim blur of movement out in the shadows at the side of the house. One of Gerder's men had gained a position down there, and he ducked behind a wheelbarrow in the yard, firing again. Drake leaped for the door.

He shoved against it and hurtled inside, catching at the inside knob to keep from falling, slamming it shut. Then he saw Midge, crouched against the couch, her face pale and tearstreaked. Simms turned from where he had his hands on her shoulders.

"She wouldn't go," he panted, and blood was

leaking from a scratch above his eye. "Fought like a wildcat. . . ."

"Drake." She had risen to her feet, stumbling past Simms, and was in Drake's arms, sobbing against his chest. "I wouldn't go without you, I couldn't, don't make me, please don't make me. . . ."

"It's too late now anyway," he muttered, feeling a momentary anger, "they're around back," and then the anger was gone, because he couldn't feel that way, with her, and he tried to make his smile reassuring, holding her away so she could see it. "That's all right, honey. They aren't getting you, understand? I'm here and they aren't getting you."

The thunder of Etienne's gun filled the room suddenly, from where he had been crouched at one of the slot-like windows, and he spat through the opening. "Paillard. That will teach you to try and sneak down my porch. A twenty-eight gauge on the bottom and a thirty-eight caliber on the top, and all you have to do is tell me which one you want."

His LeMat pounded again, and Drake sprawled across the couch beneath the other window, throwing his words over one shoulder to Waco. "Get to the back. If you need help, yell."

Simms helped his wounded boy through the kitchen door, and that would be two of them back there. Out the window, Drake could see the huddled form of the man Villeneu had shot trying to cross the porch. Drake became aware that it had gotten darker in the room, and he twisted around to see Midge turning down the last oil lamp, plunging the room into darkness. Then he sensed her moving toward him, and she kneeled on the floor beneath where he was half lying on the couch. Her small hand settled onto his back, warm and soft, giving him confidence, somehow, and it made him smile, because he had been trying to think of something to say that would comfort her, and he realized it had been she who had comforted him. There was some movement in the cotton-woods, and then a group of men broke from the trees farther up the road out of range, moving toward the barn. They disappeared behind the barn, and after that a silence settled down.

"Simms, everything all right back there?" called Drake softly.

"Yeah," said Simms. "What they up to?"

"Don't know. They muffed a try at rushing us from the front. Etienne got one of them for your boy at the fence."

"Thanks," said Waco. "I hope I get the same chance. It sure is quiet out there. Gerder's up to something. You want to watch it, Drake."

Drake realized he was perspiring. It wasn't particularly warm. Waiting? That was probably it. Waiting for what? He found his hand aching from the force of his grip on the Winchester, and tried to relax it. Midge shifted against him, and he could hear her breathing. Etienne moved restlessly on the other side of the door.

"*Sacre*, why don't they do something? It makes me more nervous than watching a Yankee try to eat Macaroni *a la Napolitaine*."

Drake shifted farther forward on the couch. The moonlight lay brightly across the compound. The Tanques Verdes rose somberly above the sweep of meadow, silent, waiting. Everything seemed to be waiting. Drake saw the blueroot north of the house flutter faintly in a rising breeze; then even that stopped. He licked his lips. Midge must have risen enough to look over his shoulder and see it about the same time he did, for she took that last breath sharply.

"Drake, it's piled with hay."

They had wheeled his linchpin wagon from the barn, dripping with the hay Simms had hauled in from Tucson for feed. They had a pair of Drake's heavier horses in the harness. As if it had struck both of them at once, Drake turned and found Etienne looking at him.

"They can't," he said, "not an adobe house. It won't work."

"Your *portales* aren't adobe," said Etienne, "And neither is your roof. If it strikes the front here, the wood of the overhang will carry it right into the roof proper, and *voila*"—he threw a kiss at the ceiling—"*finis*."

"Drake!" Midge's voice held all the terror of

sudden realization. "You mean they're going to smoke us out?"

"They're already doing it," he said, nodding toward the wagon. The first flames had begun to lick up the pile of hay in the bed, and a man was mounting the front seat. He got the horses going, turning them toward the house, and when they were breaking from their trot into a gallop, jumped off. Several other riders were on either side of the team, shooting into the air and lashing at them with quirts, but it was the fire that finally completed the job, sending the team into a frenzied run as they felt the heat on their rumps and heard the crackling flames. Drake levered his .30-30. "Try to down those Morgans before they reach the house. Never mind the men. It's our only chance. Get back, Midge. Hit this front wall and they're liable to cave the whole thing in."

His shots drowned his voice, and the riders dropped away from the running team to let it go on, the flaming linchpin careening behind, swaying from one side to the other and trailing burning hay in its path. The pair of Morgans was silhouetted against the fire, and Drake saw one of them leap up in its run as his third bullet struck. But it didn't down the animal. The horse kept stumbling along, trying to tear free of the harness, pulled on by its frenzied mate. Drake could hear Etienne's LeMat bellowing, and he snapped home his lever for the last desperate time, firing again at the wounded horse. He heard the animal scream again, and saw it fall against the other Morgan, and then go down. But the other horse couldn't stop, and the uneven pull swung the wagon around.

"Drake," screamed Midge, pulling him back off the couch, "Drake!" and he stumbled and fell on top of her as the back end of the wagon completed its half circle and smashed into the support in front of the window Drake had been using. The support collapsed beneath the driving weight of the loaded wagon, and the tailgate smashed on in under the *portale*, thundering into the adobe wall with a force that shook the whole house. Flaming hay showered in through the window, and the wall sagged inward, ripped by a network of deep cracks.

Drake leaped forward, trying to beat the fire out before it caught on the harateen covering of the couch, but the blaze above had already started, the spruce frame of the *portale* catching immediately. The ceilings of these adobes were formed of interlaced boughs laid across the *viga* poles forming the rafters, with earth piled on top of that; the boughs were woven so closely that no dirt seeped through, and all that was needed to seal it from winter rain was a succeeding layer of adobe plastered on top of the earth each spring. But already the spruce of the porch's overhang was burning, and flames licked in

195

through the walls, climbing down the inner *vigas*.

"We can't stop it now!" shouted Drake above the crackling flames. "This is what Gerder wanted. We'll go out the window, on the west side of the kitchen . . . that's the shortest run to the timber."

He caught Midge around the waist with one arm, pulling her toward the kitchen door. The roof was already covered with greedy lanes of red fire, and a flaming bough disengaged itself from the interlacing sections, burned off at one end, dropping across Drake's shoulders. With a strangled little cry, Midge tore it from him, beating his smoking shirt with her small hands. Drake pushed her on through the kitchen door, turning to see Etienne charging across the front room as one of the hanging blankets went up in flames and fell across the heavy pier table at this end of the room. The whole front wall back of the couch was a mass of flames now, and a *viga* pole crashed down behind the Frenchman as he reached the kitchen.

"They're waiting out there," he gasped. "All around, Drake!"

"Take this," said Drake, shoving his Knuckle Duster into Midge's hand. "My father used it when he worked the boats on the Missouri. I guess you know what to do with it."

"Was your father a gambler, too?" she said. Then she looked up, and there was near hysteria in her giggle. "That's a silly thing to ask at a time like this, isn't it?"

"All right, all right," he told her, taking hold of her elbow. "We're going to get out of this, understand."

"I'm not afraid, Drake," she said, and the hysteria was gone.

Drake looked toward Simms, crouching at the slot-like kitchen window. "How is it?"

"Gerder's out there with maybe half a dozen," said Waco, licking his lips. "Most of them behind the bunk shack. One or two in that ditch you been irrigating your corn with. They must be crazy. They must know they're just as liable to hit the girl as . . ."

"Shut up," snapped Drake.

"Never mind, Drake," said Midge. "I know how it is."

Another *viga* crashed down behind them in the front room, and the roaring of the blaze forced Etienne to raise his voice. "If we're going, we better start right now, Drake. That fire'll reach the kitchen in another moment."

Drake looked at Waco, and the lean foreman nodded. "You with the girl. I take it first. Then Jiner here. How about it, Ji?"

The wounded man nodded grimly, hugging his shoulder with the same hand in which he held his six-shooter. Waco broke open his gun, spun the cylinder, then snapped it shut. He had his free hand on the window sill when someone shouted from outside.

"What are they saying?"

"Gerder," said Waco. "He says you can come out with your hands up and empty, and they won't shoot."

Drake met his eyes. "You aren't in this, really, Simms. Why don't you put your gun on the kitchen table?"

A disgusted look entered Waco's acrid face, and he spat, and crawled through the window, and his gun began banging from outside. Grimacing with pain, Jiner let Etienne help him through, and then it was his weapon going, too. Drake took one last look at Midge, and his lips worked across his teeth in a lop-sided grin, as he turned to crawl across the thick sill. Bullets were thudding into the adobe as he dropped outside, and he stood with his back against the opening, closing it off till he felt Midge's head against him. Jiner and Simms had thrown themselves prone on the ground and were firing steadily at the cottonwoods, and it was the only thing that saved Drake from being riddled against the wall of the building. Unwilling to face the hail of lead Jiner and Waco were throwing, Gerder's men kept to the cover of the trees. But as Drake moved forward to let Midge drop out behind him, still shielding her with his body, he saw the shadowy movement in the irrigation ditch. His lever made a sharp, metallic click, and the Winchester bucked against the hip. At the same time, he saw the man's gun flame, and his head jerked back to a terrific blow on his neck, and the blood pulsed hotly beneath his shirt.

The moonlit landscape spun before him; Midge's arms were around his body, keeping him from falling back. He could see again by the time Etienne had gotten through the window, and the man made a crumpled blot across the heaped earth banking the irrigation ditch.

"All right?" said Waco, not looking around.

"All right," said Drake. "Make for the ditch. It leads past the cottonwoods almost to timber. I think I got one of the men in it."

He was already running forward when he realized only Waco had risen, and he faltered, looking at Jiner. Waco threw himself for the ditch, shouting hoarsely: "Never mind, he got his packet, no use stopping."

The roll of gunfire was deafening now. Drake dived for the ditch with Midge, spitting out mud and dirt and rolling to his knees in the shallow bottom. Waco was already crawling down the ditch, firing at the movement near the end. Drake saw the man, too, and pumped a shot at him. There was a loud splash, and the firing from up there stopped. They crawled through the water single file, passing the man Drake had shot from the house; he lay silently across the heap of earth banked above them. Then they came to the second man, face down in the water, and he moaned softly as Drake crawled over him. From out in the cottonwoods, Gerder began to shout.

"Cut across the end of that ditch, Italy! They're trying to reach the timber. Throw your men between the end of that ditch and the trees."

"Gerder!" shouted Waco hoarsely, and rose from the ditch ahead of Drake to fire. But his six-shooter only clonked on an empty chamber. Drake did not know whether he heard the shot first, or saw Waco jerk, silhouetted against the sky like that, or whether it came all at once. Waco bent over with a hollow cough and slid back into the ditch. By the time Drake reached the ramrod, Waco was sucking in air painfully. He tried to laugh, and blood clogged in his throat.

"I'll blow smoke out my short ribs every time I drag a fag now, won't I, Drake? No, don't try to help. I'm done. I won't have to worry about fags. Just load my gun for me, will you? I'll get it empty again before I step on my last horse. Load my gun."

Drake could see how it was, and he thumbed the .44 shells from Waco's belt, getting the man's blood all over his hands, and punched out the empties in the big Peacemaker and stuffed in the fresh loads. Then he slipped it into the hand Waco had been holding across his chest, and that was wet with blood, too.

"It was a good ride, Waco," said Drake, a hand on the man's shoulder.

"Get going, damn you," gasped Waco, and then crawled up the bank and deliberately stood erect. "Here I am, Gerder!" he called out. "Here I am, damn you, and there's one for Andy." The roar of his Peacemaker drowned him out.

Drake had already dragged Midge on down the ditch, and he heard her sobbing, and felt like it himself. They reached the end of the gully to see Italy's men moving in from the other side.

"My turn, *mon ami*," said Etienne, shoving by Drake, and jumped out of the ditch before Drake could stop him, opening fire with his LeMat. Drake saw one of Italy's men fall sideways. The rest was a madness of roaring guns and shouting men and pounding feet. Drake knew abstractedly that Midge was yelling with the best of them and shooting the Knuckle Duster, and that his own Winchester was empty.

"*Sacre bleu!*" he heard Etienne shout once, and then he realized the first spruce trees were closing around them, and they were in the timber. He dropped a little behind Midge, panting, dizzy with the pain of his wound, reloading his Winchester from the box he had in his pocket.

Etienne's boots thudded heavily through the timber behind them, and then made a soft padding sound as they struck the carpet of needles beneath the first pine. Drake quartered them on

201

the slope instead of going directly up, so they could run faster. Suddenly Midge went to her knees in front of him.

"Can't go any farther, Drake," she panted, crying with utter exhaustion. "Can't run any more."

Drake picked her up in his arms, stumbling blindly on up the slope at an angle, rattling through some plum bushes. He didn't know when he became aware that there was no sound behind him. Turning, he couldn't see Etienne. Chest heaving, he moved blindly back down-slope, trying to approximate the direction they had come in. Etienne had fallen in some gumweed. Drake set Midge down and pulled the Frenchman clear, turning him over on his back.

"I'll never forgive you for that, Villy."

Etienne smiled wanly. "I thought if I didn't call, you might not know it, and go on. You were a fool to come back. No, don't try to move me."

Drake remembered, then, that last time Etienne had yelled. "Gerder?"

"*Oui*, Gerder, I think. I was running like a jack rabbit, and I don't know for sure, but I think it was Gerder. Jack rabbit?" He raised up with a sudden violence, and Drake could see the delirium in him, with all that pain. He began to writhe from side to side in Drake's arms, his voice becoming a thick babble. "That reminds me, Laramie, I think I'll have *Filets de Levraut a la Mornay* tonight. Two young leverets, *compre*? Young hares, about"—he surged up against Drake, holding out fat hands to measure it, staring at them with wide glazed eyes—"about so big, *hein*? *Oui. Filets* of two leverets. Then prepare the same number of bread croutons as there are slices of the filet, *compre*, and the same number of sliced truffles." His breath was coming in hoarse, swift gasps now, and his head dropped back against Drake's arm as his babble became almost incoherent. "*Oui*, the same number of sliced . . . sliced truffles. Cook them in two cups Madeira, then add the filets and croutons, colored in clarified butter. *Compre*? After that add a little juicy pale glaze and sauce and sautéed slices and serve it in a hot timbale. And *voila*! Filets of young hare . . . Young hare . . . *Mornay*. . . ." He lifted his head with a great effort, and for that last moment the delirium seemed to have left him, and there was only a faint, final surprise in his eyes. "*Sacre bleu*," he mumbled weakly, "you let me finish."

Midge had gotten to her knees beside them, and as Drake gently lowered the fat Frenchman back to the ground, she spoke in a strained whisper. "Drake, is he . . . ?"

"Yes." Drake's face held a sick, gray color. "Villey has cooked his last rabbit."

VIII

With the first heat of morning sun, a ground fog steamed out of the sodden earth on these northern slopes, not yet dry from the rain of several days before, and the tall junipers dripped dew into the banners of milky haze swimming about their hoary feet. Drake's mind was a blank when he first awoke, except for a dim sensation of throbbing pain in his neck. His body was so stiff he could hardly move, then he felt the soft weight of a body against him, and it began to come back. They had been forced to leave the dead Etienne Villeneu unburied there on the foot slopes, driven away by the oncoming Gerder and his men. Carrying Midge half the time, Drake had managed to elude them finally, seeking the ridge tops above his Double Deuces valley. Lying there now on the soggy bed of needles where he had thrown himself when he could go no farther, the gambler gently shook Midge.

The same blankness he had felt was in her blue eyes, and then the memory, sweeping through and turning them wide and dark. She began to tremble against him, and he did not know whether that was reaction or cold.

"I've caused you so much trouble," she said, and began to cry softly. "Your friends in town, your house, Waco and Etienne, everything you held dear. . . ."

"I've still got something," he said, his fingers tightening on her arm. He could see the utter despair in her and knew this, if any, was the time to tell her. "I've got you, Midge. I don't know why I was afraid to face it before . . . the way I feel about you. I kept trying to tell myself you were a kid. I guess that's natural enough. I guess that's the way most men my age would react at first, when they began realizing how they felt about someone fifteen years younger than they were. Sort of a perverted defense against something they never met before. But I'm through trying to say you're a kid. You're a woman. You've got all the maturity a man could ask. Villey seemed to know how you felt about me."

"He *did,* Drake, he *did.*" Some of the despair had left her, and he saw the same look in her face that had been there when she was asking about Donna, and he knew why she had asked now. It filled him again with that sense of holding something infinitely fragile, and he was almost afraid to breathe.

"What does age matter," she murmured. "There's no fifteen years' difference between our minds, Drake. There's no difference at all. They work alike and think alike and feel alike. We enjoy the same things, we hate the same things, we love the same things."

"Yes," he said, "we do," and her lips were sweeter than Donna's had ever been, or any other woman's, and, somehow, it was different than it had been with Donna, or any other woman. Finally he got to his feet, helping her up.

"We aren't through yet, Midge. We'll still finish this fight holding the high card." He patted his shirt. "I sent Simms into town after that fifteen thousand. I've been wearing it in a special belt under my shirt ever since. We'll see Colorado Carnes on time."

He had used up all his Winchester shells, and had been too weak to carry the useless rifle as well as Midge, but the girl had retained his Knuckle Duster, with three .41 shells still in it. He tried to use it for hunting something to eat, but his neck wound nauseated him so much he could hardly see. In time Midge found some creosote bushes, and using one of the wind matches he carried to light his pipe, built a fire of dry cottonwood, heating the creosote leaves and forming a pulpy poultice that she tied onto his neck with her bandanna.

"It's an old Indian remedy," she told him. "You'll be surprised how much better you feel in a little while."

There was no outfit in the Tanques Verdes between Drake's Double Deuces and Apache Gap; the nearest privately owned land they could reach from the Double Deuces was the strip flanking Cochise Ridge that Hazard owned, but Hazard's house was miles south of that. Thus, without hope of horses, they set out to foot it all the way to the Gap, crossing the ridge above them and dropping down the other slope. They were nearing the bottom when Midge caught at Drake's arm, halting him with a hissing intonation.

An old game trail cut through the black cotton-woods below them, and the riders had rattled the leaves of a low branch, passing by. Barton Gerder came first, on his dappled gelding, whey-bellied and big-rumped from the grain in Ansel's livery stable. Behind Gerder was Kirkboot, Hazard's big, ugly foreman. Then Italy, his black derby mashed in on one side, his left arm in a sling. Finally it was Sheriff George Kennedy, on a gaunt mare as glum and sour as himself. Drake and Midge stood rigid, motionless, not twenty feet from the riders as they passed. Just before he was out of sight, Gerder turned his black-hatted head to look up the ridge. Midge's hand tightened in Drake's but Gerder had been looking through a lane of trees to their right, toward the crest, and was gone before he saw them.

"They look like they could use some sleep," said Drake. "I'll bet they've been riding all night like this. Gerder's a clever man. He knew we'd have to come down from the top lands sooner or later. He's probably got some more men riding the ridge."

"They'll see us if we try to cross the valley." Midge's voice was tight.

"We'll never make the Gap on time if we wait here till night," said Drake. "Game?"

She drew in her lips, nodding her head. They crossed the game trail, seeking the thickest stands of timber. This western slope was in shadow, but as soon as they crossed the narrow valley and began to climb the opposite slope, the sunlight picked them out pitilessly as they moved upward through the fragrance of the pine, and before they had sighted timberline, Drake heard the first shout from the ridge across the valley, small and clear, significant enough. He could see the riders on the crest over there, and was high enough to see Gerder's movement on the lower slopes, a shadowy, glittering impression through the green pines. As Drake and Midge topped their own ridge, they could see the riders crossing the valley and rising through the slopes beneath them. Just beyond the top, so they wouldn't be skylighted, Drake turned parallel to the crest; far ahead, now, he could see how this ridge melted into the sheer cliffs of the Gap. The girl knew more about trailing than Drake, and she showed him how they could cross shale without leaving tracks, and utilize fallen timber with the same success. Perhaps, not knowing they were heading toward the Gap, Gerder had expected them to keep on the same route and drop into the next valley, and had lost time looking for their trail to follow the slope down. At any rate, they reached afternoon without sighting him again, but the threat was always there, driving them when Drake would have liked to rest for Midge.

By dusk they were stumbling through the timber of the top lands near the Gap, stupid with exhaustion, their clothes and skin alike ripped by catclaw and serviceberry. They reached a small stream trickling down from a hidden source higher up, and Midge dropped to her belly to drink, and then lay there, too weary for even the movement that would satisfy her gnawing thirst.

"We have to stop here," said Drake. "Gerder or not, we've got to rest a while." Then he was on his knees beside her, scooping the water up in his hand for her to drink.

He must have dozed, or sunk into a stupor, for the next consciousness he had was of an owl hooting mournfully from the timber above them, which stretched its dark pattern across a yellow moon.

It was worse, trying to find their way by night through the tangled thickets covering the slopes to the escarpment above Apache Gap. Finally, they topped Cochise Ridge, and squatting there in the chill, they could look down on the old shack tucked down in a hollow on the slope that ran into Hazard's Big Hook. There was an ancient corral in ruins behind the shack, but no sign of life.

"Funny," said Drake. "Colorado called it a trapper's cabin. I never heard of a trapper building a pack pole corral like that. Looks big enough for a whole string of ponies."

His mind was not on that, however. It had been a trying journey, but there had been a goal to carry him along. Now that they were here, with so little time between them and the end, he felt an abrupt let-down, and for the first time, the doubts swept him. Would Colorado come? He had banked so much on this; it was their last hope, really. And if Colorado came, would what he brought solve all this?

As had happened so many times before, Midge seemed to sense his mood, and her hand slipped into the crook of his elbow. "Don't worry. I know you can't trust Colorado, but he'll be there. He isn't the kind to miss fifteen thousand dollars for anything. And he must have something we can use. I don't think he'd have the nerve to try and pull a switch on you, Drake, to your face."

"Listen," he said, turning to her, and this was difficult for him. "Listen, there's no telling what will happen down there, or what's waiting, or what will come. You . . ."

"No, Drake." Her voice was sharp with a rising fear. "No. I've come this far. I'm in it as much as you. I'm not afraid as long as I'm with you, Drake, but if you left me . . . up here . . ."

He drew a heavy breath, muttering—"All right."—and moved toward the cabin.

Moonlight cast a deep pool of shadow beneath the west wall, enigmatic, mysterious. The silence threw its weight against Drake. His hand was sweating around the Knuckle Duster's engraved brass frame. He pulled his index finger from the trigger guard to release the sliding safety lock beneath the frame. Holding Midge's fingers with his other hand, he quartered down the hill, leaning against the slope. His boots knocked some shale loose, and its clatter was startling in the stillness. Colorado had told them dawn, but there was no telling when he would arrive. They walked tensely across the level before the cabin, the shadows reaching out greedily for them. Then Drake heard the groan from within, and it startled him into a sick nausea like a sudden blow in the groin. He had stopped so abruptly the girl brought up against him, and the two of them stood rigid, holding their breaths without knowing they did it.

"Colorado?" whispered Drake.

"Colorado?" The voice boomed from within the cabin like an echo. "That you? Come back here, damn you. You're out there, come back here and kill me. Least you can do that. Not going to lay here two, three days with this hole in my belly. Hear me? Come back and get it over quick, will you? Least you can do that. Damn you, Colorado, come back and kill me. . . ."

"Binder!" Drake had recognized the strange mechanical tones. "It's Drake, understand? It's Drake out here. I'm coming in. Don't do any shooting if you planned to. All right?"

"All right." Binder's voice held a flat rage. "Hurry up, that's all."

Drake stumbled over an upturned stool near the door, saw Binder's legs sticking into a yellow beam of moonlight that slipped in a wide crack through the east wall. Drake almost went through a rotten place in the floor before he reached the man.

"How did you get here?" he said, going to his knees beside Binder. "Colorado shot you? He's been here?"

"Tell you if you put me out of my misery," grunted Binder. "Hell couldn't be any worse than this. Colorado contacted me in Tucson, told me to meet him here tonight with twenty thousand, and he'd give me the deed to land controlling the Gap."

"Sort of shuffling his cards fast," said Drake. "He made a date to meet me here tomorrow morning on the same deal . . . though he didn't actually mention the deed."

"Probably planned on having me out of way by the time you arrived," said Binder. "He had the deed all right. One of those old federal homestead patents issued under the territorial legislature."

"Then Colorado owns the Gap . . . ?"

212

"He doesn't own anything," said Binder peevishly. "He was a fool to think I'd buy the deed off him like that. When I refused, he put a load through my belly and took the money anyway."

"But if he doesn't own the Gap, who does?"

"You, Drake," said Colorado Carnes from the doorway. "You."

IX

Colorado's flat-topped hat held that cocky slant against the black silhouette of his thin head, and the way he held one narrow shoulder tilted beneath the other told Drake on which side he carried the heavy Springfield.

"Don't move any more," Colorado said, then laughed briefly. "That's it. I didn't expect you so early, Drake. I thought I'd have our P.R. friend out of the way by the time you came. When Binder saw the deed, he tried to get cagey. I don't like cagey characters. A Springfield Thirty makes a nice hole through a man's belly. I'd just gotten the money off him when I heard your horse nicker down in the Gap. Those cañon walls throw an echo you can hear a mile off. I couldn't hide Binder. He was still alive, and he might have groaned or something, and I couldn't shoot him again for fear you'd hear the shot. I went out to try and meet you before you hit the shack. I found your horses down off Cochise Ridge. You must have taken a different route than I did."

Drake sensed Midge stiffening beside him. "But we didn't . . ."

"What did you mean the deed was mine, Colorado?" interrupted Drake swiftly. Horses down off the ridge? That was the only chance they had now. "I never owned land here."

"Face Card Farrow had no living relative, and your partnership with him wasn't dissolved legally at the time of his death, consequently you now possess Face Card's estate," said Colorado. "Part of said estate is the deed. It was among his papers."

"You were the one who killed him," said Drake.

"In a little argument over back salary. Face Card had been sorting his papers, and I thought I might as well sweep it clean. You should have seen the stuff I got, Drake. Enough to hang half the men in Tucson. The deed had belonged to Midge's father, Edward Lawrence. Lawrence came here in 'Seventy and staked his homestead on Cochise Ridge. The quarter section runs right down off the ridge and crosses the bottom of Apache Gap, controlling the eastern entrance to the Gap. This shack isn't a trapper's cabin like everybody has gotten to think . . . it's Edward Lawrence's original home."

"That's why Gerder was after Midge," said Drake. "He thought Midge had the deed."

"Yes." Something tense was entering Colorado's voice, and he leaned forward as if to peer at Drake's face. "Lawrence moved from here before Midge was born, and I guess she, like everyone else, thought her dad sold this quarter section to Hazard along with the rest of Cochise Ridge. That's why she didn't know what Gerder wanted from her. Gerder was Lawrence's ramrod at the time, and he was the only one who knew Lawrence kept the original homestead site. But what Gerder didn't know, when he found out the P.R. would pay twenty thousand for that site, was that Lawrence had signed it over to Face Card Farrow for a gambling debt. Now give me that money you brought, Drake."

Drake was staring past Colorado, trying to see any movement out there now. "How did you figure the Gap came into my hands, Binder?"

Perhaps Binder sensed the game, for his answer came deliberately. "Face Card Farrow had already approached P.R. about selling the Gap, but by the time I arrived in Tucson, he was dead. As his partner, I knew the deed would go to you if he'd possessed it."

"And Farrow had you kill Edward Lawrence," Drake told Colorado.

"I'm warning you, Drake," said Carnes. "If you don't give me that money, I'll shoot you right here on your knees. I don't know what you're stalling for, but if you . . ."

"Face Card knew that whoever possessed that deed was in a dangerous position. The Tucson Cattlemen's Association would just about commit murder to keep that deed from falling into the hands of P.R." The sweat was dripping into Drake's eyes now, as he saw the strained line come into Colorado's long body. "So in order to keep his acquisition of the deed secret, Face Card had you kill Lawrence that night after Lawrence had left the Coronado House."

Binder was playing along with Drake now. "It's funny you didn't know all this before, Drake, as Face Card's partner."

"I didn't handle the table Lawrence played at that night," said Drake. "And I left Face Card's politics strictly alone."

"Drake . . ."

"All right, Colorado." There was something final about Drake's voice. "I'm through stalling. They're so close together; they're knocking each other down now. As Midge started to tell you, we didn't come on horses tonight. Those were Barton Gerder's horses you found off the ridge. And that's Barton Gerder coming over the ridge behind you."

"Don't try to pull that old one on me, Drake," said Colorado.

Gerder must have thought it was Drake standing in the doorway, because he had come over the ridge top and down the slope and was within easy range now, just past the corral, when he called: "Just keep standing right there in the door, Drake, and drop whatever you have in your hands!"

Colorado stiffened, then twisted around, shouting: "It's me, Bart, not . . . !" Then the deafening smash of guns cut him off, and the hail of lead literally carried him halfway across the room. His body dropped heavily across Drake's and Midge's, where Drake had thrown himself against the girl, knocking her sprawling on the floor. After the rolling echoes had died, they could hear Gerder's voice.

"You'd better come out now, Midge. Drake was a damned fool to try it that way. We don't want you to get hurt."

"They won't shoot you, Midge, they want you alive," said Drake, trying to fish the Springfield out from beneath Colorado's bloody body without sound. "But there's no telling what they'll pull when they find out that they didn't get me. Sooner or later they'll find out, and sooner or later they'll force us out of here. We might as well make the first move. Tell them you're coming out, and not to shoot."

She hesitated a moment, staring at him, then spoke in a strained voice. "I'm coming out, Gerder. Don't shoot. . . ."

He shoved the Knuckle Duster into her hand, and rose with Colorado's Springfield and the man's cartridge belt unbuckled from around his waist. He drew a deep breath, then moved straight toward the doorway.

"Stay here, no matter what happens," he hissed. "It's our last draw. Now tell him not to shoot again."

"Don't shoot, Gerder, I'm coming. . . ."

Drake was out the doorway into the moonlight then, and he had taken his one step toward the corral, raising its dilapidated skeleton to one side of the house before someone up on the slope across the compound shouted: "Hey, that's not Midge, that's a man!"

The surprise of it held them an instant more, and Drake had already thrown himself bodily toward the corral posts before they opened fire. He rolled across the open compound with slugs thudding into the earth all about him and brought up hard against a pile of grass-topped sod that had built up along the broken fence through the years. Then he was sprawled on his belly behind the sagging corral with the Springfield across the bottom bar and over his sights he could see two of them exposed on the slope, trying to scramble back up to the cover of the ridge. He swung the rifle till the bulk of one man was square across his front button, and it bucked up hard against his face, and he saw the man spread-eagled in the air for that moment, and then fall over backward and roll down the slope. Drake snapped the bolt open, the hot shell popping out, and thumbed in a fresh

.30-30 from the belt. But before he had it in the breech, the second man had topped the ridge, silhouetted there for one maddening moment while Drake snapped shut the bolt and tried to raise the gun all in one movement, and then had dropped back on the other side before he could fire.

It didn't matter much. They knew he was alive now, and out of the cabin, and whatever they did, they wouldn't be shooting at the cabin, so Midge was safe there.

"Kill me, damn you!" shouted Binder from within the shack suddenly. "Drake, come back here and kill me!"

"That you, Drake?" It came from the ridge, Gerder's voice.

"Yes, Gerder," said Drake. "That Berry I got just now?"

"No, it was Kirkboot," said Gerder. "He was the only one of Hazard's bunch that would stick with us. You blew Jack Berry's legs off with that shotgun back in Tucson. I'll make a deal with you, Drake."

"Any deal you make will *have* to be with me, now," said Drake. "Midge hasn't got the deed to this quarter section. She never did have. Her father signed it over to Face Card Farrow, and it's mine now."

There was a pause while Gerder digested that. "I'll give you fifteen thousand for it," he said finally.

219

"What about Hazard?"

"Hazard's out of it. He wouldn't dare buck you with that proof of his connection with the Corral Street fire in the marshal's hands. Hazard had himself appointed the girl's guardian to get his hands on that deed and keep P.R. from ruining the Tanques Verdes for cattle by diverting the water in Apache Gap. Hazard thought by having the girl around he'd find out what her father had done with the deed sooner or later. He was afraid to question her directly for fear she'd tell someone else what he was doing. I got fed up with the cat-and-mouse game and tried to force it from her that day she was out riding."

"You mean you wanted to get the deed before Hazard did and sell out to P.R.," said Drake. "The only reason you threw in with Hazard is so he wouldn't buck you on Corral Street."

"What does it matter? Hazard's out of it now. Whether his connection with the fire comes out now or later, it doesn't matter. He's through in the Tanques Verdes. The T.C.A. will dump him out of the saddle as soon as they find out how he's been driving his cows. It's just you and me now, Drake. Fifteen thousand. Enough to set up a new Double Deuces for you."

"You'll have to go higher than that, Gerder," mocked Drake. "Did you think the P.R. hadn't already reached me? They offered me twenty thousand. Can you and Hazard meet that? I wouldn't take it if you could. I'm no girl, to treat the way you treated Midge, Gerder. It'll be a little different trying to take that deed off me. Why don't you come and get it, Gerder? That's the only deal you can make with me."

Drake realized he had been talking a long time without any answer, and he wondered if Gerder hadn't kept the palaver going to cover something. There was only one way they could approach him without exposing themselves. The shack was in a cup-like hollow, with Cochise Ridge taking a half-circle curve above it in the front. One end of the curve was across the level compound from Drake, but the near end overlooked the corral. With a swift decision, he got to his hands and knees, slinging the cartridge belt over his shoulder, and began crawling down the dilapidated pack pole fence to the rising ground. There was a shot from across the way; lead kicked dirt into his face. But that did not mean someone else wasn't working down the other side of the ridge toward him.

He crouched behind the last pole of the corral, then shoved his leg out and drew it back. The shot came from the ridge across the compound and he fired between the bars at the flash. Then he threw himself in a run up the slope toward the ridge top on this side, reloading as he ran, and his shot had held the man over there down long enough so that Drake was almost at the crest before the firing began again. He stumbled to the top and threw himself across the talus to roll into a pocket on the opposite side, out of sight of the shack. He did not know he had been hit till he tried to rise, and his leg went out from beneath him. He felt the sob begin way down in his throat, and it was more anger than pain, and he stopped it before there was any sound. Then he began to crawl along the ridge. There was growth here, and the air was heavy with the scent of night-blooming cactus, its white flowers forming large pale splotches all down the slope on this side to the very lip of the cliff that formed the sheer side of Apache Gap.

Drake sank into the deep Texas crabgrass behind a screening clump of barrel cactus, and this was where it would be. He had jammed a fresh load into the breech, and he shoved the bolt home slowly, silently. He knew the man across the compound had been covering someone's move-ment over this way, and it would not be long. The pain of his leg began to intensify, and he found himself gritting his teeth. Then it was the noise. Not much at first. Not enough to attract a man, unless he had been expecting it, or waiting. Drake had been waiting. He licked his finger and ran it over the sight at the end of his rifle, and the sight gleamed wetly in the moonlight. The barrel cactus was not enough to hide him. Whoever was coming around the curve of that ridge would see him about the same time he saw them. He wished he could stand for this, somehow. He drew himself to a sitting position, propping the gun across his knees. His last thought was of Midge. At least they would hound her no longer.

"All right, Gerder," he said.

But Gerder had already seen him. The man stiffened there atop the ridge as his gun hammered, and the lead clattered through the barrel cactus and slammed through the wooden stock of the Springfield with stunning force, knocking the gun up, and it was all Drake could do to keep his finger from pulling the trigger spasmodically. Gerder jumped down the slope, throwing down to fire again. Drake jerked the Springfield back into line, and for that instant, the wet front sight gleamed across the dark bulk of Gerder's belly, and Drake squeezed the trigger. He did not see Gerder take the bullet. All he saw was the man continue to crash down the slope in that headlong run, and his instincts would not wait for more, turning him spasmodically to the noise above and behind him. His twisting motion threw him on his side with rifle pointed directly up at Italy, who had just risen on the ridge above, a six-gun up by his head to throw down on Drake. Italy stood that way for a long, rigid moment. Then he dropped the six-gun down his back, moving the arm he held in a white sling. "You winged me back in Tucson, shooting me off the horse," he said. "I guess that's enough."

"Kick your six-gun down here," said Drake, and when the man complied, he snapped open the breech of his rifle, and the hot, fired shell popped out. "Didn't you ever see a single-shot Springfield?"

Italy made a small, frustrated movement toward him, but Drake had already gotten the six-gun. He turned to see what had happened to Gerder; the man was not in sight. Italy spoke finally, and the frustration was in his voice.

"Bart ran right on down the slope and off the cliff with your slug in his belly. I guess the P.R. will find him when they divert the Río Caballo."

"The P.R. isn't going to divert the Río Caballo," said Drake. "Any more of you?"

"The sheriff. I had to hold him on the other side while I was trying to keep you by the corral so Gerder could work above you over here."

"George," shouted Drake, "are you going to come out now, or will I have to get you?"

In a moment the sheriff came stumbling down the ridge. "I'm not in this, Drake. I didn't know it was like this. Hazard only told me he was after you because you took Midge. When I found out what Gerder was really after, I tried to stop him."

"I know, George," said Drake wearily. "I know. But now Gerder's out of it, and maybe Tucson will settle down a bit and you and Petrie and a lot of other fence-sitters can come down and have a beer with your friends again. Now help me back to the shack. I got a packet in the leg."

Midge ran from the cabin as soon as she saw them helping Drake down the slope. Binder shouted at them as they carried Drake toward the door.

"Now you've killed all the others, maybe you can get around to me. Swear if I have to stand this one minute longer, I'll blow my top."

"You aren't going to die any more than I am," groaned Drake. "Sheriff's going to get the horses and we'll take you back to town. I've seen men with more lead in them than you live to a ripe old age."

"Damn you, Drake." Binder sucked in a resigned breath. "How about the deed? The girl found it on Colorado, along with some other papers."

"It's still not for sale," said Drake. "I'm going to run cattle in the Tanques Verdes and I want water for them. Hazard had the right idea about that, but he was pulling his cards from a cold deck. My cards aren't marked, and they're laying face up on the table."

"P.R. is a mighty big organization. . . ."

"You told me that once," said Drake.

"As I said, P.R. is a mighty big organization. But I've been with them a long time. They'll take my judgment on things. When I saw you walk out of Tucson with that shotgun, I figured you were going to be a hard man to beat. When I heard how Gerder burned down your house and you still didn't quit, I figured you were going to be almost impossible to beat. When I saw you go out and take Gerder tonight, I knew you couldn't be beat. Think I'll wire P.R. that they better start surveying that other route around the Tanques Verdes."

Kennedy had paused in the door before going to get the horses. "Looks like your fighting days are about over, then, Drake. All that's left is getting a guardian for the girl. I don't guess Petrie will put up a fuss about that now that Hazard's taking the trail out."

"It won't be necessary," said Drake.

"How's that?"

Drake was looking at Midge, and it was more for her than anybody else when he said: "A girl doesn't exactly need a guardian when she has a husband, does she?" He saw the answer in her eyes.

THE TETON
BUNCH

I

Victor Bondurant opened the door without knocking and stepped in, closing the portal behind him and standing against it. Lamplight glittered across the sheriff's star on his hickory vest and caught the quick, perceptive flash of his vivid black eyes. The strange scars scoring his jaw had always given the narrow, calculating intelligence of his face an ineffably vicious look.

"Not knocking any more, Victor?" said Gordie Hammer, from where he sat at the table.

Bondurant's flannel mouth began to curl at one corner, like a lazy snake, into that slow mocking smile. His right hand lifted from where it had hung above the white bone butt of the big Forehand & Wadsworth sagging with such studied casualness at his negligible hips. The light made a brazen flash on the $20 gold piece held with ironic delicacy between his thumb and forefinger.

Hammer stared at it a long time before the expressions began seeping into his face. A strange pain flickered through his wide brown eyes, and a small muscle quivered into view down his heavy-boned jaw. His broad lower lip stiffened outward till the even line of clenched, white teeth was visible, and he drew a heavy breath through these that lifted his deep chest up against the soiled denim shirt he wore.

"It popped up down in Kemmerrer," said Bondurant. "Nearest we could trace it was to a saloonkeeper who couldn't remember the drunk. Double eagle, Gordie, minted in 'Eighty-Two, only six hundred and thirty of them issued. Maybe you know the story." His voice had taken on a thin sarcasm. "The whole issue was allotted to the paymaster at Fort Laramie. The government made the mistake of sending it by stage from Cheyenne to Laramie. They sent a troop of cavalry under Captain Bill Bondurant to take it off the train and escort it through, but that didn't make any difference to the Jackson Hole Bunch. They were a wild crowd, Gordie. They drew the troops off and jumped the stage at Eagle's Nest Gap. Even got the money off before Captain Bill got on their tail."

"Victor!" cried Hammer, unable to stand it any longer. He had stood without feeling himself rise. He had been going over his books and his strong, spatulated fingers were pressed so hard on the ledger their tips showed white. He stood that way a moment, seeking some control, and when he finally spoke again, his voice was husky and strained. "When will you stop riding me, Bondurant? How many times do I have to tell you I don't know where that money is hidden?"

"And you didn't kill Captain Bill Bondurant." It

was as if the sheriff had finished it for Hammer. Victor Bondurant walked across the room toward the bed, sending one quick sharp glance to either side that took in everything, and turned about, his eyes resting on Hammer again to study him from beneath the sardonic arch of his brows. "You know when I'll quit riding you, Gordie. When I find out where you have that money, and when I find something to convict you of murdering my father. Maybe Kelly figures you've paid your debt to society, spending ten years in jail for complicity in that robbery. I don't. And maybe the jury couldn't find you guilty of murdering Captain Bill. I do." He held the coin up, staring at it with the cruel little lights coming and going in his brilliant eyes. "It's inconceivable to me Kelly can be so easy on you, Gordie, seeing as he was the lieutenant riding stirrup to stirrup with Captain Bill at the time. Even close enough to hear what that man said at the tail end of the Jackson Hole Bunch when he turned and shot Captain Bill." His lips barely moved around the words now, and his voice was hardly audible. " 'Ain't that nearly hell,' he said, 'Gordie . . . ain't that nearly hell. . . .' "

The light threw Hammer's shadow across the wall in a warped, lean-shanked, heavy-shouldered copy of his figure, stiffening as he did, till the top touched the shadows in the rafters. His breathing formed the only sound for a moment hoarse, strangled. He wondered how much longer he could contain himself. Bondurant's narrow head raised in a small jerky motion, and his tongue made a sly flick across his mobile lower lip.

"If you didn't drop this coin in Kemmerer, Gordie," he said, "that would mean one of the others was back, wouldn't it? Eden, maybe, or Makwith. If they were, what would you do, Gordie? 'Hello, Makwith, glad to see you back, thanks for leaving me there when my horse got burned down. I served ten years for it, but that doesn't matter, glad to see you back, we'll go and get the money now and split it up . . .' "

"Victor . . ."

It came from Hammer, sounding as if someone had their hands on his throat throttling him, and one of Bondurant's sardonic brows raised in mock surprise. "You're trembling, Hammer." His laugh was short, harsh. "How you've changed since you were a kid. You didn't have such wonderful control over yourself then. So wild, so unbroken." He allowed his eyes to wander momentarily over the high-ceilinged room, the heavy pegged furniture, the grizzly pelt before the stone hearth. "But then, I guess it would take that kind of a change to get what you've got here. Not many men could come back and build a spread like the Big Dipper with everybody just waiting for one wrong move. Little outside money must have come in handy on the rough spots, ah, Gordie?"

Hammer's move toward Bondurant contained a

spasmodic violence, but was halted abruptly by the sound outside the house. It came sharply through the door, in a lull of the wind, the thud of hoofs, the creak of saddle leather, then the portal shook to someone's fist. Hammer's lips twitched stiffly about the words.

"Come in."

Edmond Kelly had the stiff, mincing walk of the inveterate horseman whose girth had grown with the years, but who still retained the lean, bandy legs of a man used to the saddle. His fleshy face was whipped the color of raw beef by the wind, and the furrows in his jaw turned pale white when he tucked his chin in with a characteristic gesture to give the whole room one swift, lashing glance from his glacial blue eyes. He tugged off one rawhide glove and beat his palm against the leg of his corduroys to remove some of the numbness.

"Fortunate you're here, Bondurant," he said. "Hammer's cut my fence again and half a hundred head of E Kay stuff has drifted off into that chasm in the Snake."

"Again!" said Hammer, stung to thoughtless reaction. "You know that storm drifted it down last month, Kelly, you said so yourself. . . ." And then the import of it struck through his anger, and he stopped, staring at Kelly, the breath stirring his heavy chest more swiftly. Kelly's foreman had come in. Lister Birgunhus was an immense Swede with tremendous hands made more for the huge battle-axe of his Viking ancestors than for the curved butt of the Frontier he packed. His blond hair hung tousled down about the shoulders of his thick plaid Mackinaw, and a long pale mustache drooped into a dirty yellow beard.

"We thought it was an accident last time maybe," he rumbled. "But we saw the wire this time, Hammer. It had been cut and pulled aside."

"I've tried to be decent with you, Hammer," said Kelly, his words coming out in clipped, angry gusts. "I wasn't any happier than the others to have a jailbird for a neighbor, but I tried to give you the benefit of the doubt. I've over-looked a lot of little things all along, but this snubs the dally." He turned partway to Bondurant, moving his hand in a vicious gesture. "I want you to do something about this, Sheriff."

Bondurant's smile curled up one corner of his lips. "Some legal action might be taken if you have proof it was Hammer."

"The fence is cut . . . my cattle are dead at the bottom of the cliff. What more proof could you ask?" snapped Kelly.

"That's only circumstantial," Bondurant murmured.

Kelly bridled like a spade-bitted horse. "Cir-cumstantial, hell! You and half a dozen others know Hammer has wanted that south forty of mine for its winter shelter ever since he came here. How many offers for it has he made me in your presence? How many of his Big Dipper beef have been found drifted over there through that fence?"

"That's still not strong enough for me to do anything, Kelly, you know that," said Bondurant, flipping the coin.

"Then I guess it's my hand." Kelly's voice had lowered to a tense, restrained scrape, and he took two mincing steps at Hammer, till their faces were but inches apart, and his protruding girth touched Hammer's belt. "What are you going to do about it, Hammer?"

Hammer's big hands had closed. "I didn't cut your fence, Kelly, but I'll go out and repair the cut like I did last time."

"That won't quite be enough, Hammer. Do you think I mean to go on playing this kind of game forever? You cut it and I'll let you patch it up and you cut it again. How could you possibly conceive that this would get you the pasture? Just because I lose a few head of cattle and some of yours drift through? That's such a childish way, Hammer, I can't quite believe that's your real motive. This offer to patch the fence is so childish, as if that would end the whole thing."

"What else can I do?"

Kelly moved his face closer. "You can get out, Hammer." It was so unexpected that Hammer felt himself draw up, unable to answer it, and Kelly's next words struck his face as a hot breath. "I told you I'm not chewing this hay over a third time. If you can't think of anything else to do but patch that fence, I can. And I'm doing it. You're getting out, Hammer, one way or the other, and if you won't go of your own accord, I can always force you."

"Don't be a fool, Kelly. . . ."

"Don't call me a fool," snarled the man, flushing, and his hand flashed up to crack twice against Hammer's face, backhand and forehand. The spots showed red in Hammer's pale face, gradually disappearing into the pallor again as Hammer stood there with his whole body trembling like an asp in a heavy wind. He felt the terrible, driven desire for violent reaction but he could see them all waiting for that—Kelly bent toward him with that one hand still held up, Birgunhus grasping one glove with the other ready to bare his own gun hand the instant Hammer moved. Bondurant's brows arched in hopeful expectancy.

For a moment Hammer could not see with that black wave of violence sweeping up in him, and all the years of careful deliberate, terrible restraint threatened to be smashed. Without actually seeing it, he was aware of his own Remington in its holster with the gun belt wrapped around the scabbard, lying on the table, and his right hand twitched. Then gradually, before his awesome exertion of will, that blackness receded, and Kelly's waiting face swam into view before him again. Bondurant emitted a rueful little breath, looking at the coin as he flipped it.

"Maybe you're wrong, Kelly," he said. "Maybe you can't force him."

II

The snow had hidden the drift fence in most places, piling up in haunted white mystery, but cattle had trampled it down about the cut section, and two or three posts stuck up here in shorn loneliness. They kept their horses heavy on grain during the winter to stand the cold up here, and the shaggy, steaming flank of Hammer's roan held a padded resilience as his leg slid across it, dismounting. He stood staring at the cut fence, trying to consider the possibilities in the light of a cold calculation that came hard to him, with that terrible, frustrated rancor still gnawing at him. Yet he felt a dim satisfaction at not having allowed Kelly to force his hand back there. It would have been the worst thing he could have done. With Bondurant just waiting for some overt act on his part to jump him, it was what he had fought against and guarded against so many years now.

He turned to his pack animal and unslung the bale of barbed wire, unrolling it in the snow. He could find no clear motive for anyone deliberately cutting the fence. If Kelly really wanted him out, perhaps the man had opened it in hopes of engendering a clash that would result in Hammer doing something that would put him in Bondurant's hands. Yet that was not consistent with Kelly's attitude during these years. The man was too blunt for something like that. Hammer had torn off the old, rusty wire, and was pounding the third brad into the east post when the sense of another presence stole over him. He turned slowly to see her.

It was Irish hair, blue-black as a Colt barrel, hanging in a long, curling, untrammeled bob about the milky line of her neck. There was something nebulously sensual about the small crease that formed in the plump flesh of her chin when she tucked it in that way, and her heavy-lashed eyes seemed to hold some deep, mysterious, slumbering capacity in their dark blue depths. It had always inspired a strange awe in Hammer to look into them, and the words came from him in a hollow whisper.

"Carey Shane."

She wore a heavy canvas Mackinaw with a sheepskin collar and a pair of man's blue jeans, and she dismounted like a man, with a lithe, casual swing of one leg, her eyes on him all the time. She bent forward to study his face narrowly, taking in the grooved lines that had formed about the thin restraint of his lips, the weather creases at the corners of his eyes that imparted to them such a withdrawn, calculated look.

"You've changed, Gordie," she said in that husky, whispered way he remembered so poignantly.

"Bondurant was right, then," he said. "Makwith is back."

A dim, harried look passed through her eyes at the name, and she dipped her head in a short nod. "The old spot in the park. He'd like to see you."

"Isn't it sort of dangerous there," he muttered. "They detailed a troop of U.S. cavalry to police the park in 'Eighty-Six."

She shook her head. "We haven't even seen them. You know nobody ever comes in those hills north of Old Faithful."

He shrugged, and mounted. They reached one of his Big Dipper line shacks on Jackson Lake in a couple of hours, and he turned the pack animal into the shed behind. Then they followed the shore around to the Snake again, and took the river north toward the park, cutting across to Belcher River and following it up through Silver Scarf Falls where a slate gray water ouzel hopped unconcernedly about on the slippery rocks and dived into a foaming pool. Carey had kept sending him those covert, sidelong glances all afternoon, and finally he could not retain it.

"So you stuck with him," he said at last.

Something tightened the planes of her face. "He's my husband, Hammer," she said, and the simplicity of it would have struck him harder but for the sense of something else moving behind her words, something she could not quite hide from him. Up past the falls they turned west from the river through a saddle in pine-covered slopes and dropped into the geyser area. They passed small pools of boiling varicolored mud and a small geyser spouted steam on their left. Soon the ground began to tremble perceptibly beneath their feet.

"That's Old Faithful," muttered Carey. "She goes off about every hour. The cabin's near enough to shake each time."

They left the trail and cut into meadows of snow and into deep stands of blue spruce. The cabin stood in a dell, hidden from all sides by this heavy timber. Legend held John Colter had built the shack when he first discovered Yellowstone and brought back stories that caused the park to be called Colter's Hell. The structure looked old enough for that, with its blackened logs. With a quick, unreadable glance at Hammer, Carey dismounted first, and turned to push open the door. He was close enough behind her to hear the crash of a chair inside, and then could see the man who had jumped up from where he had been sitting, hands gripping the worn oak stocking of a rifle so tightly the bones protruded whitely against the gnarled flesh.

"It's just Carey, Makwith," said the woman in a pleading way.

Makwith Shane lowered the gun reluctantly. He was gaunt to the point of emaciation, and his straggly mane of black hair, shot with gray, only accentuated the ravening, wolfish appearance of his face. There was no flesh to fill the starved hollows beneath his prominent, Indian cheek bones, and his eyes gleamed bloodshot and feverish from their deep, skeletal sockets. It was such a violent change from the laughing, reckless, vivid youth he had known that Hammer could not quite hide his shock, and Makwith saw it.

"All right, all right, what did you expect?" said Makwith viciously. "A stinking government man on my tail all the way up from the Red River and nothing but the lousiest crow bait in Texas for horseflesh and a damned whining woman nagging my tail off twenty-four hours a day. . . ." He broke off, a strange, cunning light flashing through his eyes, and his narrow, gaunt head dipped in a sudden, obsequious way. "Hell, Gordie, I shouldn't pop off like an old squaw on an occasion such as this, should I? I'm sorry as hell, after thirteen years and I jump down your throat the first minute. It was just you surprised me, that's all . . . here, sit down." He lifted the chair back on its feet, shoving it toward the table, and turned toward Carey. "Make us some coffee, will you, honey?"

Hammer cast a glance at Carey, still not quite seeing how it was, and then took the chair. Makwith leaned the rifle against the stone fireplace and lifted a three-legged stool across the plank table, bending forward to put his elbows on the rough pine boards and study Hammer. His mouth twisted in a warped grin, revealing yellow, decaying teeth.

"I understand you're a big rancher hereabouts, now, Gordie. I have to hand it to you. It must have been an uphill grade."

"It was," said Hammer, glancing at the greasy leather *chivarras* on the man's skinny legs. "Texas?"

"Yeah." Makwith's laugh was harsh. "Mex leggings. They all wear 'em down there." He jerked his head at a flat-topped Mormon hat setting at the end of the table. "Utah, too. Oh, we've been traveling, Gordie." He bent forward sharply, eyes strange and bright on Hammer's face, speaking swiftly. "That's why we couldn't get to you, Gordie. I would have sprung you, believe me. I would have moved heaven and earth to get you out, but God, they wouldn't let me be, I had to keep moving all the time. Carey and me been on the bob ever since. Thirteen years, Hammer, running all the time, why in hell did you have to pick a soldier to burn down?" He stopped abruptly, seeing the mistake of that in Hammer's face, and held out a bony, grasping hand placatingly. "Ah, I didn't mean that, Gordie. I know it wasn't your fault. It was dark and you were jumpy."

Hammer's lips worked faintly against his teeth, and he held himself from answering with an effort, back stiff against the chair. Carey came over with the coffee pot and some tin cups, staring from one to the other in a wide, dark way.

"All right," said Makwith, waving his hand at her. "Gordie and I want to talk. Get out."

Carey's lips pouted. "But, Makwith . . ."

"You heard me," snarled Makwith, half rising. "Get out!"

"It's cold outside," said Hammer. "I think your wife has a right to hear whatever you and I have to talk about, Makwith."

For another moment Makwith remained out of his chair, face twisted in that wolfish snarl. Then servility returned as his glance swung to Hammer.

"Sure, Hammer, sure, what could I be thinking? You see how jumpy I am, hell." He poured a cup of coffee. For a moment the spout touched the rim of the cup, making a small, staccato rattle. Makwith jerked it up with a guilty look. He shoved the cup to Hammer, poured himself one. He took a quick, furtive gulp, watching Hammer over the rim of the cup. There was a palpable effort to the casual sound of his words. "I guess it would have been nigh onto impossible to make a go of it without that money to tide you over the rough spots, hey, Gordie?"

"What money?" said Hammer.

Makwith's laugh held that same furtive effort. "You never used to be a joker, Gordie."

"Neither did you," said Hammer.

Makwith sobered abruptly. "I'm talking about the fifty thousand golden eagles, you know that, now quit hiding things in your poke, I'm serious. I had my ear to the ground. It came over the grapevine, the things you had to buck up here, Bondurant, and the way Edmond Kelly and his bunch tried to squeeze you out at first. I didn't call on you then because I knew I didn't really need it, but now you're sitting on top of the horse, and I'm the one who needs it, Gordie."

"Needs what?"

"The money, my share," said Makwith impatiently. "There was four of us, wasn't there? Eden is dead now so we split his fourth. Has Dee Sheridan hit you for his yet? The last time I heard, he was up in the Tetons somewhere."

Hammer bent toward the man, studying that gaunt, ravaged face. "Are you trying to tell me, Makwith, that you think I have the money?"

"Think?" Genuine surprise lit the man's bloodshot eyes momentarily. Then a sly, growing malignance turned them a strange yellow tint. He leaned forward on his elbows. "Gordie, don't act like this, even if you're joking, I'm in no mood for it, can't you see how bad I need that money? You was the one got those bags off the stage, we all know that. I was up on the rimrock, holding them off with my rifle. I saw you do it."

"And the bags were on the back of my horse when Bill Bondurant shot it from under me," said Hammer.

"Sure, sure, and they wasn't there when we came back next day and found the animal," said Makwith. "I never did understand how you found time to cache them bags."

"I didn't have time," said Hammer. "The horse slid off in a gully. I hadn't even got to my feet by the time the troops came up."

"But the money was gone, Gordie, the troops didn't find it, we know that."

"Someone else must have doubled back for it," said Hammer. "They've been dropping those eagles here and there ever since. One showed up in a bar at Kemmerrer a little while ago. Did you come through that way, Makwith?"

The man took a quick, sharp little breath, straightening up. "You mean you think I got . . . ?" He cut off, slamming both palms flat on the table so hard it trembled and, rising to his feet, his voice rose to a shrill stridor. "Listen, Gordie, I told you not to talk this way. I know you got that money and I want my share. The others'll want their share, too."

"I haven't got it."

"You have!" shouted the other, rage turning his face livid.

"Makwith, please," said Carey, catching at his shoulder.

"Let me go, you damned trollop!" screamed the man, jerking his arm free and letting it fly back to smash her across the face. Carey stumbled backward with a sick cry and crumpled against the stone fireplace.

"Damn you, Makwith," roared Hammer, kicking his chair back so it would not trip him as he rose, but his knees were still bent when Makwith whirled back and grabbed the front of his open Mackinaw, pulling him down across the table with a violent jerk.

"I guess that would make you mad, wouldn't it?" shouted Makwith. "You was always sweet on her, wasn't you, Gordie? Well she's mine, by God, and I can do anything I want with her."

With his chest against the planks, Hammer twisted over in an effort to free himself, and the weight of his body upset the table. Makwith released Hammer, allowing him to fall on over with the table, and then jumped at him as he sprawled across it between the legs. Makwith struck him, screaming like a crazed animal, that greasy hair hanging in matted tendrils down in front of his eyes, lips pulled back from those rotting teeth, eyes filled with frenzied rage.

For a moment Hammer was filled with the same blinding rage, engendered doubtlessly by seeing Makwith strike Carey, the same rampant emotion he had known as a kid, and he was as abandoned as Makwith, shouting crazily at the man as they rolled across the upset table like two wild animals, biting and kicking and slugging. They came up against a leg and it snapped off beneath their weight, allowing them to roll off on the floor. Hammer caught Makwith in the mouth with a heavy blow that knocked the man partly away from him, allowing Hammer to get on his knees. Then, crouched there, seeing the terrible animal rage that gripped Makwith, realizing how it blinded a man, Hammer brought all the deliberate, careful control to bear that he had developed during these last years, stifling his own red anger in its cold fist.

Makwith threw himself on Hammer again. This time Hammer shifted his head aside in a swift, calculated way, avoiding one of the man's clawed hands, and his own hand shot up to grasp the other. With this leverage, he twisted Makwith to one side and used the man's own momentum to pull him on in, jabbing for Makwith's groin with his free fist at the same time.

The man emitted a sick, spasmodic groan, and lost all volition. Before he could recover, Hammer jabbed him there again. Then he released the incapacitated man and allowed him to roll over on his face on the floor. Hammer stood there, chest heaving, looking down at Makwith for a moment until he became aware of Carey's eyes on him. She was still slumped against the fireplace, holding herself up by a clawed grip on the rough stones, and there was a strange, twisted wonder in her face. He stared at her a moment, then he wheeled toward the door.

"Hammer . . ." Makwith's voice stopped him, and he turned his head over one shoulder to see the man, still sprawled there on his stomach with his arms hugged across his groin, one knee lifted to twist him part way over so he could look up at Hammer, and his voice shook with a hoarse, bitter, agonized hatred. "There are other ways to get that money. I could have used them first. I didn't have to give you this chance, but now there are the other ways, and, by God, before we're through, you'll wish to hell you never saw a double eagle in your life!"

III

Snow came on the wind, and to Hammer, wading through it from the barn to his house, there was something vaguely sinister about its nebulous, powdery touch, sifting insistently against his face and sticking his eyelids shut. He shook his head in a small, growing irritation, stumbling on the stone steps of his front porch, pawing for the door handle. A thin sliver of yellow, as tall as himself, appeared before him, quickly growing into a large rectangle. Partly blinded by the snow, he could not comprehend it for an instant. Then he realized he had opened the door to a lighted room.

"Crazyjack?" he called, thinking perhaps that one of his crew had come in from the line shack for something. But the ramrod did not answer, and he pawed his eyes free at last to see the room was empty. Then its round, yellow gleam caught his eye, lying on the top of the table beneath the sputtering camphene lamp. It should not have shocked him so. Yet it did, somehow, filling him with the sense of small, chill fingers spidering along his spine. With a muttered oath he stepped to the table, picking up the coin. Then, insidiously, the face seemed to rise before him, the vivid black eyes filled with that cunning, waiting intelligence, the odd, haunting scars grooving that sharp, vicious jaw, the mocking, fluid, curling smile.

"Damn you, Victor," he said in a guttural voice.

"Victor Bondurant?" asked the throaty voice from the doorway.

Hammer had not realized how tense he was till he whirled that way. Carey Shane stood there, blinking snow-fringed lids, taking off her mittens. Hammer felt the little muscles twitch in his cheeks, and he took a heavy breath, striving for relaxation.

"Is he still riding you, Hammer?" she said compassionately, coming on into the room.

He gripped the coin, a speculation sending its cold shaft through his mind suddenly, and his eyes narrowed. "I don't know."

"That's the reason you've done it," she said. "This change," she said. "I saw it at first, and didn't recognize it. I saw it again tonight, with Makwith. For a moment there, when he first jumped you, it was what you used to be, Gordie, so wild and abandoned, without any control. Then, suddenly, that control. I guess you've had to, haven't you, with Bondurant riding you, all of them riding you, just waiting for one wrong move?"

His hand kept opening and closing on the coin. "I guess so."

She came up to him suddenly, one hand on his chest. "Why, Hammer, why do they do it, why can't they let you alone, haven't you proven your sincerity by now, can't they see what it was by now? You were only a wild orphan kid running in the wrong kind of company. They've made mistakes, too. Won't they ever realize how many times over you've paid for yours?"

"Bondurant still thinks I killed his father," said Hammer.

"How can he be such a fool?" she said hotly. "It was so dark and confused and so many shooting there."

"It's that expression the man used just before he shot Captain Bill Bondurant," Hammer

250

muttered. "You don't hear it much up here. 'More to the south, Kansas, or Oklahoma.' Some say Sam Bass used it. There were two or three troopers right behind Captain Bill. Edmond Kelly was one. They all heard the man call it. 'Ain't that nearly hell,' he said, and then shot Captain Bill."

Her lips formed that rich petulance, and light rippled blue-black across the angry toss of her hair. "That doesn't cinch any saddle. Just because you knew Sam Bass down on the Red River. They haven't any right, Hammer. . . ."

"It doesn't matter," he muttered. Then he raised his eyes to hers. "I'm not the only one who's had a rough time. How did you get out?"

She shrugged uncomfortably. "You know how Makwith drinks. It put him to sleep."

He slipped the coin in his pocket to catch her shoulders. "Why do you do it, Carey? Surely, you can see by . . ."

"He's my husband!" she blazed, her chin snapping up. Then, with her eyes meeting his, he saw the tears forming in them, and suddenly she was in his arms, sobbing against his chest. "Oh, I don't know, Hammer, maybe I don't love him any more, you can see how he's changed. He's not right in the head any more. He gets those rages, you saw him, he drinks so much now, he's so sick, Hammer, in the mind, in the body. He does need me, doesn't he, tell me so, Hammer, he'd be dead without me? I just had to make my choice,

251

that's all. Maybe I don't love him like I used to, how could a woman? But I can't leave him now."

He tightened his arms around her, seeing for the first time all the hell she must have endured these last years, knowing the same rended emotions he had felt so long ago when he first realized how he felt about her, and how he could never have her as long as Makwith was alive.

At first he thought the camphene lamp had flared up, to flicker their shadows across the wall that way. Then he realized the source of light was coming through the opened door. The shrill whinny of a horse, muffled by the snow, reached him. Carey pulled away, tear-stained face turning up to his, and then whirled in his arms to stare out the door.

"Your barn, Hammer," she gasped. "It's on fire!"

The drifted snow clutched at his feet with every step he took and threw a blinding white blanket before his eyes and fell in small clouds from his shoulders with every violent movement of his body. His other horses had started screaming now, and one began kicking at the walls as Hammer reached the door, catching the edge and throwing his weight outward against it to heave the portal open. With a bursting roar, flames licked redly into his face, and he staggered back, shouting in pain.

"Hammer, Hammer . . ."

"The fire's all along the front," he cried to Carey, "my back door's locked. The loft is the only way left. Find me that ladder. I can't see. It might be out by the pigpen."

Pawing at his singed brows and burned face, he went after the sound of her pounding feet in the direction he thought was toward the corner of the building, only to smash headlong into a splintery wall. It dazed him, and he had to hold the planks to keep from falling.

"I've got it, Hammer!" cried Carey, and he could see dimly from one tortured eye now, as the woman appeared from the powdery snow, dragging the heavy ladder. He helped her stand it against the building, and then climbed up, tearing open the loft door and bellying over into the hay. The flames had eaten through cracks in the loft floor, and he gagged on the odor of smoldering hay. The ladder on the inside was already burning and he had to hang and drop. He went to his roan first, fighting its head down in the stall to tie his bandanna about its eyes, battered against the sides by its violent thrashing. Finally, he got it backed out of the narrow confines and headed toward the rear door.

He kicked the bar from its sockets and put his shoulder into the door, swinging it open. Carey was there to catch the roan as he came through, and he tore the bandanna off its head and wheeled back in after the next animal. It was a black stud he had rented from Kelly to service two brood mares, and it had already smashed the bottom out of its closed box stall with its wild thrashing.

"Ho, boy, ho, big boy," he called to the beast, trying to keep his voice soothing, but the moment he unlatched the gate and swung it open, the animal turned on him, screaming and rearing up. He dodged in, fighting to avoid its vicious front hoofs and get the blind on, but the stud was in a blind frenzy. It broke forward before he could pull its head down, smashing out the open gate and running headlong toward the flames.

Hammer had just stumbled free of the stall when the horse, feeling the heat of the fire, wheeled back this way with a crazed whinny and charged down the aisle.

"Hammer, watch out!" he heard Carey scream, and then his whole consciousness was thrown into the shuddering impact of the animal against him, and he had a dim feel of spinning off its shoulder and crashing into the side of the shattered stall and falling. It was all blackness with no relative objects to give him any sense of motion, yet it was there, regardless, that nauseated sense of spinning—around and around and around. He heard hoarse groaning, and his feet seemed to be getting hot. Then his shoulders twitched, and he realized someone was tugging at them. The groaning turned into muffled, animal sounds as he tried to help them, his face buried in the dirt and hay.

"Gordie, Gordie, try to get up!" sobbed Carey. "You're too heavy to carry and it'll be on us in a minute, please, Gordie, please . . . !"

Things were coming back more sharply now, and he heard the crackling roar of the fire behind him, and understood that heat on his feet. He managed to get to his hands and knees, then, with her help, to rise. Carey pulled one of his arms around her shoulder, and together the two staggered out. Carey must have opened the pigpen to let the pigs out, for they made dimly running, grunting shapes all over the compound, and the roan was trotting in a frightened, nervous circle farther out. Free of the blazing barn, Hammer stopped and turned to look.

What framework of the front end was left, formed a bizarre, charred pattern that appeared momentarily in the crimson holocaust. The rest of the building would be gone in a few moments.

The wild scream of those brood mares and his pack horse came to Hammer through the crash of falling timber and roar of flames, and his throat knotted up with a small, inarticulate sound of pain as he made a vague move back toward the barn.

"Gordie," said Carey, catching him, "you can't. It's hopeless, now. You'd only burn with them!"

He realized she was right and stopped, his big figure sagging wearily. Then another realization crept through insidiously, and he turned his burned face toward her, twisted now with a strange pain.

"What's the matter, lose your nerve?" he said.

She stared blankly at him. "What?"

"Why didn't you just leave me in there?"

"Gordon, what are you saying?"

"Other ways?" His voice held a note of hysteria now, and he backed away from her in repulsion. "Sure there are other ways. Plenty of other ways. He'd started using them even before I saw him there in the park, hadn't he? I should have known it the moment Bondurant came with that coin. I should have known Makwith was back and starting in even then. It was him who cut that fence."

"Fence?" She took a step toward him, trying to read his face. "What are you talking about, Hammer, what fence?"

"Makwith!" he shouted at her in a sudden fit of rage. "He wants me on my knees where I'll have to give in to him. He was the one bargaining up there in the shack, and he wants to turn the kak around. You can't deny it. He cut that fence to bring Kelly down on me. And he sent you down here to hold me in the house while he burned the barn. You can't deny that."

"No, Hammer, no," she sobbed, jumping forward to catch his arm, "don't be a fool. I told you, he's back in the shack asleep, how could you believe I'd do a thing like that?"

"I *do* believe it," he told her, tearing loose. "He needs you? You're damned right he needs you. To do all the dirty work he can't do. You make a good pair. You always did. I spent ten years in jail for the two of you. Makwith wasn't the whole reason I ran with the bunch. Now get out, Carey. Don't touch me again. I'd be afraid of what I'd do." His big work-roughened hands were opening and closing spasmodically. "Get out, and, by God, you'd better hope *we* never meet again!"

IV

Crazyjack stumped heavily around the living room, doing unnecessary little things like straightening a tattered rug that didn't need it and moving the box of Remington flat noses from one end of the mantle to the other. He was an old ranny as grizzled as a bighorn's antler with a patch over his right eye and a baldpate that shone like a slick horn. The Big Dipper could not support a large crew yet, and though Crazyjack was no more ramrod than the other two men, the combination of age and experience had always caused Hammer and the others to consider him in that light.

"Colter's Hell, Hammer," he growled, knuckling the gray stubble on his furrowed jaw peevishly. "I don't see why you have to pick this time of year to go breaking brush up north."

"Do you think I've got that money?" said Hammer, bent over his bedroll.

"Don't be a jackass," snorted the old man.

"They think I have, Crazyjack, and they won't stop riding me till I prove I haven't . . . Bondurant or Makwith or Kelly or any of them . . . and the only way I can prove that is to find out who has got it," said Hammer. "Somebody must know where it is. Those double eagles haven't been popping up by themselves all through these years. With Makwith ruled out, that only leaves Dee Sheridan. Makwith said Dee had last been heard of up in the Tetons. I know a few of his old pastures."

"Why not let me trail along then," said Crazyjack. "With the cards stacking up the way they are, it ain't too safe for you to be running around alone. I keep thinking of that Bondurant."

Hammer's face lifted, and he stared for a blank moment at the fireplace. Then he tucked his chin down again, jerking the tarp around his bedroll. "I need you here. I've fixed it with Leese to give you power of attorney. You can draw on my account in Jackson to pay next month's grain bill if I'm not back by then, and the mortgage. Take that stud back to Kelly and don't let the shotes lose any weight."

He drew the last lashing tight around the tarped

roll and rose and stepped to the table, lifting his Remington off and unwinding the belt from around the slick leather scabbard. He opened the box of flat-noses on the mantle and began stuffing the .44s into the cartridge loops on his belt.

Crazyjack's voice was somber. "It's funny, Hammer, but this is the first time I have seen you wear that."

Hammer paused, his eyes taking on that blank lack of focus. "I didn't want to pack it for fear of what might happen, Crazyjack. I hoped never to use it again."

The old man made a vague, snorting sound and stamped over to scoop the tarp off the floor. Together they went outside. Crazyjack slung the bedroll on the roan behind the saddle and lashed it tight for Hammer. Then the two men turned to each other, clasping hands. Without speaking again, Hammer turned back to slip the ground-hitched reins over the animal's neck and climb aboard.

He reached Jackson that evening, halting his tired roan in the slushy snow before the Hoback Saloon. He had talked with ranchers and fence riders all the way in without hearing anything he could use, and was beginning to feel discouragement. He shoved through the batwings of the Hoback and moved through the sticky sawdust spread on the floor toward the bar, almost reaching it before he recognized the ponderous blond man bellied up to the mahogany. Lister Birgunhus must have seen the expression on the barman's face, for he turned with a glass of beer in his hand. His eyes caught on the toe of the holster protruding from beneath Hammer's Mackinaw. He set the glass down.

"Please, Hammer," said the bartender. "I just got new lamps put up."

"Forget it," said Hammer, moving up to the bar. "I understand you've got in some new Grandad."

"Yeah," said the barman vaguely, moving to get the whiskey without taking his eyes off them.

"What are you doing so far north?" Hammer asked the Swede.

Lister wiped foam carefully from his mustache, eyeing Hammer warily. "Repping for Kelly."

"I thought the limit of his drift was way south of here," said Hammer.

"A few E Kays were found in the Bar D stuff up in the Tetons," said Birgunhus. "I had to come after them. Bar D boys are busy cutting sign for some high rider's been working their stuff over."

Hammer took the glass from the bartender and twirled it slowly to hide his mounting interest. "Just one?"

"They don't figure any more," said the Swede. "Only a few head gone at a time. Got his pasture narrowed down to Teton Pass. Even spotted him there last week. They say he forks the biggest lineback ever foaled."

"Hammer," called the barman, "don't you want the Grandad?"

But Hammer was already to the door, pushing through, because nobody else would ride a buckskin that size, or choose Teton Pass in the wintertime. He swung aboard his roan and turned it down the street. A man came from the livery stable across the way and watched him ride out.

The pass lay west of Jackson, and Hammer began climbing a few miles out of the town, leaving the barren crowds of aspen quaking along the banks of the Snake and rising into the snow-laden spruce and pine. A luteous moon rose from behind the phalanxes of barren rock-ribbed peaks and threw the drifts into blinding relief. It was close to midnight when Hammer pulled over a ridge above timberline, passing through a short talus saddle in the granite crest. There was a slight turn in the saddle that put his profile toward the direction he had come. He could not actually see the slope he had climbed. It was only a dim sense of movement in the bluish shadow of a snowbank.

He halted his horse below the saddle and dismounted, crunching through a frozen surface back to where he could overlook the slope without being seen from below. He waited a long time before the movement came again, much farther up this time. It was farther to the north than it had seemed the last time. By that line of direction, Hammer estimated it would strike the top a few hundred yards down where another saddle cut through the sharp ridge. For a moment, he had the impulse to go on, and had even turned back for his horse. Then he wheeled back, tugging at his right glove. He could afford to spend the time it would take to make sure.

He traversed the ridge on his side, keeping below the top, and had his glove off and stuffed in his pocket by the time he reached the saddle. He glanced wryly at the hand, flexing the thick, spatulated, rope-burned fingers stiffly. They had once been so slim and supple. He drew a breath between his teeth, wondering.

Then it came, the small scuffling sound from the saddle above him, and he wheeled up that way, moving toward the cover of a granite uplift ribbed with frozen snow. He had not quite reached it when the man appeared in the saddle.

They saw one another about the same time, and had both done the same thing, and then stopped, and it came from Hammer in a hollow, strained way. "Bondurant!"

The sheriff's mocking eyes dropped to Hammer's hand, and a smile curled the corners of his lips. "I wondered who would have been left in the kak this roundup."

Hammer glanced involuntarily at his hand, still,

gripping the butt of his gun. He lifted it away, flexing calloused fingers, then raising his eyes self-consciously.

"Maybe sometime we'll find out," said Bondurant. He had been leading his big half-Morgan mare and he pulled her in to him. "Lucky you kept your temper smothered with Kelly, back at your house, Hammer. You have an amazing control over yourself. He was just waiting for one wrong move from you, with me there."

"You didn't seem so eager," said Hammer bitterly.

"I wasn't," said Bondurant. "I was glad you controlled yourself, Hammer, though I don't see how you did it. I don't want to haul you in on some minor charge of Kelly's. When I get you, it's going to be for good."

He was still smiling when he said it, that lazy, cynical smile with no rancor apparent in his face or voice. It was worse than if he had evinced his bitter hatred. It lent the words an infinite deadliness. The old frustrated anger was clawing at Hammer, and he did not speak until he could retain an even tone to his voice.

"Why did you follow me this time?" he said.

"I thought perhaps you were on the way to get another sack of double eagles," said Bondurant. "With your barn burned out you'll need some extra cash to tide you over, won't you?"

"Damn you, Bondurant . . ."

The shot cut Hammer off, loud and clear on the thin mountain air. Frozen snow kicked up with a hard, crystalline sound to the right of him. The roan screamed in startled panic and wheeled to run, striking a snow field on the slope behind and sliding down up to its belly. Hammer had his Remington clearly out this time, and threw himself toward the saddle through which Bondurant had come. The sheriff had already ducked back behind the rocks there. They crouched together, straining to see the southern ridges above them.

"Been talk of an owl-hooter cutting into Bar D stuff up this way," said Bondurant. "One of us could keep him busy here with my saddle gun while the other got out the other end of this cut and tried to work in behind him."

"You know your rifle better than I do," said Hammer, and had already begun to worm deeper into the saddle until he could move in a hidden crouch to the east. Bondurant had opened fire by the time Hammer reached the other end of the saddle. He found a gully that led him down to timber between high snowdrifts, and once in the Douglas fir he moved swiftly across the slope, through furrowed trunks standing so thickly that his elbows were constantly scraping against the old man's beard growing in parasitic malignance on the trees.

His breath steamed whitely before his face. The

shots had ceased, and it was so quiet the soft, incessant crunch of his feet began to irritate him. In the open spaces between trees, he sometimes had to crawl on his belly through the snow to keep under cover. He reached some pines with his pants and Mackinaw soggy and frosted down the front, and realized he had passed beneath the saddle through which he had crossed the ridge.

He began working up toward the higher ridges on the south side of the saddle. The firing started up again, first from Bondurant, to the north, and then above Hammer, so close it startled him. His palm was sticky with sweat from gripping the gun so long, and he wiped it against the Mackinaw under his armpit. He reached timberline and waited for the next shot. It came from a group of frozen rocks near the crest. If it were Dee, he would be too wary to stay in one place long, and Hammer stayed there. Bondurant's answering shot came. Then, after an interval, the sheriff must have showed himself purposely to draw this man's fire, for it came, even nearer this time, almost down at the edge of the rocks on this side. Hammer shifted south in a lateral line, and when he was behind the man, took a gully up out of timberline that shielded him till he could reach the scattered rocks on the crest. He saw the base of the first jagged granite uplift ahead and rounded a curve in the gully and looked up to see the man squatting in a niche with a Ward-Burton in his hands.

"I thought so," the man said, and the weapon made a deafening crash.

A terrific blow struck Hammer's left arm, spinning him part way around and carrying him back against the hank of the gully. Pinned there for that instant by the impetus of it, he saw the man snap open the gun bolt.

"No, Dee, no," he screamed, "it's Hammer, can't you see!" Then he saw the man snap the bolt shut, and, after that, it was only his instinct for self-preservation, jerking his Remington up and squeezing the trigger. Dee Sheridan stiffened, his hands twitching spasmodically, and when the Burton went off, it was pointing skyward. He hung there a moment, coughing in a hollow way. He dropped the rifle, a blank look passing through his eyes, clawing at the rock to keep himself erect.

"Well ain't that nearly hell," he said then, and fell face forward on the rock, and slid down the rough surface to Hammer's feet. Hammer dropped to his knees, turning the man over. Sheridan's shirt front was torn from sliding across the rock, and soaked with blood already from the hole Hammer's .44 had made in his chest. Then the sharp scrape above raised Hammer's head. Bondurant stood atop the rock, staring at Dee Sheridan.

"Well, ain't that nearly hell," Bondurant repeated in a soft, unbelieving voice, and shook his narrow, dark head.

"How did you get in so quick," Hammer said in a strained voice.

"I was moving in on him," muttered Bondurant. He squatted and slid down the rock on his heels, never taking his eyes off the roan. "Who is it, Hammer?"

"Dee Sheridan," Hammer told him. "I guess he didn't recognize me."

Bondurant squatted there on his heels, gazing at Sheridan in that blank way. "I hate to believe it. After all these years, I hate to believe it."

Hammer shrugged. "Dee was just as close to Captain Bill as I was, and he was working that Ward-Burton as fast as he could snap the bolt."

Sheridan stirred feebly, opening his glazing eyes to stare up at them. "Captain Bill Bondurant," he said, and giggled in a weak hysteria. "Sure." He started to cough, and blood came in little spurts from his mouth, dribbling over his chin. "Didn't recognize you, Hammer, you've changed so, sorry, sorry"—his head began to weave from side to side—"thought you was some more of them Bar D hands. I was getting tired of dodging them. Guess I was a fool to start the smoke-thrower that way but I was getting tired dodging them."

"Dee," Hammer said huskily, tugging at his

shirt. "Somebody's been passing that money. Was it you? They picked up a double eagle in Kammerer last month. Did you go through there?"

"Money?" Lucidity entered Sheridan's eyes momentarily. He tried to laugh again, failed. "Don't be loco. Think that witch would give me any of it?"

"Witch? You mean Makwith and Carey have it? It was Makwith who doubled back and got it off my horse . . . ?"

"Makwith, hell," snorted Sheridan. "He don't know where it is any more than you or I."

"Then who? What do you mean?"

"You know what I mean," he said feebly, and seemed to rouse himself for a final effort, raising up with a strangled, gurgling sound. "There's only one person in the world knows where that money is. Carey Shane."

V

They had buried Dee Sheridan beneath the snow back in the pass, and had come across his horse while getting their own animals, a buckskin at least seventeen hands high with a black line down its back, the only kind of animal Dee would ever ride. Bondurant was leading it now, behind Hammer, and with the strange growing feel of the man's eyes on him, Hammer could not help turning in his saddle.

"Ain't that nearly hell," said Bondurant. There was bitter disappointment to it.

"You'd rather I had killed your father," said Hammer.

"I would," said Bondurant. "It would make this easier."

"What?" said Hammer, and was turning once more to look at the man when he felt the rump of his roan slide to the left.

"Look out, Bondurant, you're shoving me off!" he shouted, reining the horse hard to the left. The animal's hoofs made a swift scrambling sound against the frozen rock face and for a moment Hammer thought it was all right. Then that sense of something thrusting at the roan's rump again, and the head of Bondurant's Morgan knocked into Hammer's elbow. The roan whinnied in shrill fear, and its hoofs went from beneath it. Twisted in the saddle for that last instant, Hammer saw the satisfaction lighting Bondurant's vivid black eyes, the triumph in his curling, mocking lips. Then Hammer was going down amid the wild screaming of the roan and the crash of dislodged rocks and his own helpless shouts. He threw himself inward off the animal, but Bondurant's horse was in his way, and he struck its shoulder, clawing vainly at its steaming, slick hide.

His own mount was out from under him now,

its heavy, hairy form in view for a last time, flailing through the steep slope of frozen snowbanks and disappearing abruptly over the edge into the sheer drop, its screams cut off sharply for a moment, then coming back in piercing echo from the other wall of the cañon. Hammer's own hoarse shouts drowned that, in his ears, as he felt his hands slip down the Morgan's leg and claw at the frozen snow surfaces. His torn nails crunched through the crust only to sink in slush beneath. He felt himself sliding down the steep slope faster and faster.

He caught at icy rocks and bellowed hoarsely with the agony of his weight coming against his wounded arm, and could not retain his grip. He swung his good arm out in a wild effort. His right hand crossed more jagged rocks, and he clawed at them wildly, and his fingers slipped on over their adamant surface, flesh ripped and torn, blood forming a crimson trail through the snow as he slid on down.

Then he felt the earth go out from beneath him, and heard his own terrified scream ring across the cañon and strike the opposite wall and echo back. That first release sent a clutching nausea through his groin, and then, for an instant, there was no sensation. Pain caught his leg as his foot struck something. Rocks ripped at the front of his Mackinaw again, and his hands clawed spasmodically across the rocks, once more in vain.

Something forced his feet together and his descent ceased abruptly. With his feet pinched in and no leverage there he would have fallen backward. His hands pawed blindly, catching at a granite outthrust. The weight of his body bore on his shoulder, and his twisted position tore at the muscles.

Somehow he managed to hang on, seeing that he had slipped into a shaft formed almost vertically in the cañon wall by faulting. His hands were clutching core rocks exposed in some earlier glaciation, and his feet were jammed together where the fault narrowed. Below him yawned hundreds of feet of empty space; above was the sheer frosted rock wall.

He heard the soft neigh of a horse, then the clump of its hoofs, and he knew he could not be far below the lip. He waited for what seemed an endless period, to allow Bondurant time to leave, the blood congealing on his ripped hands in the cold, his left arm stiffening up, a chilled ache adding its agony to the throbbing pain of the untended bullet wound.

Finally he could stand it no longer, and began to seek a new hand-hold higher up in the fissure. He found more jutting quartzite, and pulled himself up painfully, a few feet at a time, till he reached the end of the fissure, where the vertical face became that slanting snow-covered slope. There he had to belly over and squirm carefully through the slush that he had caused sliding down, digging sometimes five minutes before he could find another rock for a higher hand-hold. Finally he reached the trail and lay there on his stomach, a terrible lethargy gripping him.

It was a bitter fight for him to force his body onto its feet. Then he turned eastward and began stumbling down the trail. He knew there was a Bar D line shack at the east end of Teton Pass. If he could make that . . .

He had no measure of time. He did not know how long he had been staggering down the steepening trail. He lost count of the times he fell on his face. When he heard the horse snort from ahead, he did not recognize the sound, and kept right on going. Then he was aware of its dim, shying movement before him, and he opened feverish, red-rimmed eyes to see the buckskin trotting away.

"Bucky," he sobbed huskily, because Dee's horse would always have that name, "Bucky, come here, boy, come here you moon-eyed bunchquitter, oh, damn you, Bucky. . . ."

He finally reached the beast and after three tries managed to climb heavily aboard. Then he turned the animal toward the Hole and free-bitted it, knowing a dim gratitude that it had gotten free of Bondurant. It took a long time for the mutation of that thought in his reeling head, but slowly it began to change from gratitude to wonder. What if Bondurant had deliberately released the horse, to make better time? It sent a dull shock through Hammer, and he straightened up, tightening the reins and giving the buckskin his heels.

It had begun to snow again when he finally reached the valley. He had taken his left arm from the sleeve of his coat and hugged it to him beneath the Mackinaw for warmth, and now it was so stiff he could not move it. It was the fear, driving him now, that caused him to skirt the yellow pinpoints of light from Jackson and head on through the growing storm to the north. He followed the frozen bank of the Snake through Togwotee Pass to Jackson Lake. With the waters gleaming silver beneath a frigid winter moon, he skirted the lake until it ended in the Snake again. Again there was no measure of time. It was all that endless plodding through snow-robed spruce marked at shoulder height with old scars from the previous spring where the bucks rubbed velvet off their antlers.

He slept in the saddle at intervals, and lost the river several times that way. With the rising sun, he grew giddy, and was biting his lips and shouting at himself in an effort to retain lucidity. The arm felt swollen and throbbed unmercifully, and the infection filled him with the sense of coming delirium. This was why Dee had always ridden a buckskin; a man following his kind of trails needed a horse with bottom, and a line-back like this one never wore out.

He struck West Thumb's turquoise waters late in the afternoon and turned westward. He passed Black Warrior Springs, bubbling from beneath its snow-crusted shelf, melted snow constantly dripping off into the boiling water. He passed a series of small geysers, dimly aware of their hissing eruptions, and then struck Belcher and crossed into the ridges northwest of that.

Bondurant's Morgan stood hipshot in the snow outside the shack, and it was the first thing Hammer's snow-blinded eyes discerned as he topped the last ridge and dropped down the slope. Then he saw that the door was open. He half fell from the buckskin and lurched inside. It was a moment before he made out Makwith Shane lying on the floor.

The gun must have been fired from but a few inches away, for there was not much left of his face. Hammer sent a feverish glance around the room, then turned to stumble out. He searched the trampled snow about the shack till he found the line of footprints leading back around the corral and into the timber of the slope. Reaching the top, he dropped down the other slope, into a milky haze that grew thicker as he went lower. Soon he could not see ahead of him, but could still make out the tracks in the snow.

"Carey!" It came from ahead—the harsh voice of Victor Bondurant. Hammer stopped in his tracks. "Come back here, you can't get away up here."

"You shot Makwith." It was Carey's voice, farther away.

"He was a fool to put up a fight. I told him," answered Bondurant, and Hammer was moving again, toward the sound. "There's no need for anybody getting hurt now."

"Do you think I'm stupid?" she cried. "You'd kill me as soon as you got that money. It's been you all along, hasn't it? You weren't after Hammer because you thought he shot your dad. You wanted those eagles. It was you burned his barn."

"All right," he answered, and that plea had left his voice, and it was only the cold, vicious, calculating intelligence now. "Maybe I did. Maybe I cut the fence, too. I always figured Hammer used that money whenever he struck a rough spot, like the big storm in 'Eighty-Eight. Kelly bucked Hammer in the first years, but when he saw how clean Hammer was keeping his slate, he began slackening up. Even took a second mortgage on Hammer's place when the bank wouldn't. I thought if I could get Kelly climbing Hammer's frame once more, Hammer'd have to turn to the eagles again. But Hammer was a hard man. When that failed, burn him out. He did have to start after those eagles then, didn't he, even though he wasn't the one who knew where they were. Now are you coming, Carey, or am I getting you?"

"Nobody's getting her, Victor," said Hammer, as a rift in the mist opened up around Bondurant, standing in the soggy buffalo grass ahead. The sheriff wheeled, and Hammer pulled his right hand from beneath his arm where he had held it till the last instant so the fingers would be warm and supple and ready. "You wondered who'd be left in the kak," he said. "Here's your chance to find out."

Bondurant's swift recovery from the shock of seeing Hammer was characteristic. "Yeah," he answered, and went to draw his iron.

Hammer's fingers made a faint slap against the slick black top of his holster, and then their sibilant scratch, and he was out first, with the Remington bucking in his hand. The high metallic whine of a ricochet followed the explosion of the shot, and Bondurant's shout of agony. The bullet must have struck the sheriff's gun, for as the mist was swept back across Bondurant by a shift of wind, Hammer saw the man's weapon fly into the air and fall to the ground.

He fired again at the last dim sense of Bondurant there in the shifting haze, and kept running on forward, emptying his gun at the spot where the sheriff had stood. He reached the man's gun, lying in the buffalo grass, and plunged a few feet farther into the milky steam without finding Bondurant. Then a rumbling rose from beneath him.

"Hammer!" It was Carey's voice, coming faintly over the growing sound. "It's Old Faithful. Where are you? The geyser's going off!"

"Get out!" he shouted at her, going on forward, and maybe it was the memory of all those years Bondurant had ridden him, or maybe it was that terrible frustrated anger in him that he could not control this time, or stifle, driving him on in. "Get back up on the slope. He's in here some-where and I'm not leaving till I get him."

He saw a vague movement in the mist ahead and stumbled up rising ground. The rumbling beneath him assumed the steady, thunderous roll of bass drums, and his whole body seemed to take on the throb of the earth. Then, almost before seeing the man, Hammer ran into Bondurant's form.

"Gordie?" said Bondurant, and there was something close to amusement in the rising inflexion at the end of the word, as if Bondurant had been waiting there. Hammer could not see the man's face, yet the way Bondurant had spoken gave him a vivid sense of that curling, mocking smile and those bright, intelligent, waiting eyes.

He felt himself caught, still running forward,

and swung around by his own momentum, and then he knew the man *had* been waiting, right there, for his horrified eyes stared over the lip of a yawning pit into the hissing white malignance of the geyser's mouth.

Instinctively his hands clawed out to clutch Bondurant's canvas Mackinaw. The sheriff had to throw himself backward to keep from being yanked off by Hammer's weight, and this pulled Hammer's body part way back over the lip. Bondurant kicked and beat at Hammer, trying to free himself. Legs dangling into the heat of the steam, Hammer allowed himself to slide down Bondurant's legs till he was belly down on the dead gray rock forming the crater's cone.

Bondurant jerked one foot free to kick him in the face. He had to lean back to free the other foot, and Hammer released it suddenly. Bondurant staggered back in order to keep his balance, and this gave Hammer an instant to squirm farther up on the lip till his legs no longer dangled over. The incessant, throbbing rumble rose to a deafening roar beneath him, and the steam rose in a new cloud out of the geyser behind.

"Gordie, Gordie," he heard Carey's voice, somewhere way out there, as if in a dream, "it's going, Gordie, oh, my God, where are you?"

Then Bondurant had recovered himself and was lunging back at Hammer. In a violent spasm,

Hammer reached his knees, and saw the shift of Bondurant's outthrust hands upward to catch his shoulders and thrust him backward. Just before those hands reached him, Hammer dropped back onto his belly. Without Hammer's shoulders there to stop him, Bondurant went right on over, shouting something as his feet caught momentarily on Hammer's prone form, and then his shout changed to a scream of agony that became indistinguishable from the hiss of steam.

Hammer lay there on his belly, staring blankly into the pit. The ground shook with a new spasm and the steam shot up from below in a great white cloud. Gasping with the insufferable heat, he scrambled erect and stumbled down the cone with the steam roaring out behind him and scalding the back of his neck. He was almost to the bottom when Carey came running through the hot mist.

"Get out, you little fool!" he screamed.

"I couldn't stay back there," she sobbed, catching him, and whatever else she said was drowned in the last gargantuan roar. The ground shook so beneath them they could barely stand. Boiling water spilled over the lip of the crater and then the column of steam became water, rising higher and higher into the air. Staggering away, Hammer felt the boiling splash of it on his bare neck and hands, and heard Carey gasp with the pain. He threw an arm over her back and pulled her partly toward him, trying to shield her with his body. Running, they finally gained the rim of buffalo grass outside the milky fog. Here they sagged into the grass, sobbing with exhaustion, and gazed blankly at the hundred-foot column of water with its unfurling flag of steam. Finally it began to die, and the westerly wind dissipated the steam, and the rumbling ground sank to a sullen mutter.

Tears still sticky on her cheeks, Carey knelt before Hammer, clutching him with one hand and passing the other over his face in small, maternal gestures.

"I thought . . . I thought," she muttered. "Bon- . . . Bondurant . . ."

"He won't get the money now," said Hammer heavily, studying her face. "It was you all along, then."

"Not all along," she told him. "It was Eden who doubled back after the money. We had all planned to meet on the Green, you remember. But three of the troopers followed Eden into the park. His horse went out on him near Old Faithful here and he had to cache the money because it was too heavy to carry on foot. When he finally joined us, he didn't say he'd gotten the money. He planned to have it all himself. But he never got the chance. Makwith shot him in an argument over cards down near Santa Fe.

Makwith was so drunk he fell asleep soon after that, and Eden told me where the money was before he died. I knew turning the money over wouldn't alleviate your sentence any. You'd been sent up for complicity in the crime, and for one of us to give back the money would only be further proof of your guilt. Yet I was afraid to tell Makwith about it. He would have started right out spending it, and those coins would have been a clear trail right to our door."

"But those coins that did pop up," he said.

She shrugged. "I had gotten a few of them from the cache, and there were times when I just had to use one. That last one in Kammerrer. We were down to our last old boot, and Makwith was crazy for a drink. I was afraid he'd do something dangerous if I didn't get him one."

"How did Dee know you had found out where the money was?"

She shrugged. "He saw me use one of the coins about a year ago. Tried to force the location out of me. I threatened to tell Makwith that Dee had made advances or something. Dee was afraid of him. We got separated last March."

"Then the bulk of it is still up here?"

She nodded, rising to her feet. "In an extinct old geyser about five miles north."

He stood, too, drawing in a deep breath. "I feel as though a great load has been lifted off me, Carey. That money's haunted me for thirteen years now. Bondurant had convinced everybody in Jackson Hole that I knew where it was. To know that I can turn it back now, and have them off my neck, and ride down the road without feeling I'm being watched . . ." He trailed off, gazing at her a moment. Finally he began: "Makwith . . ."

"I know, Hammer, I know," she said, taking the step that brought him against her, with her face against his Mackinaw.

He put his arms about her, and they stood that way a moment. "Maybe this is the wrong time to say it, Carey, but you know I've always wanted you," he said.

"It seems I've been torn and rent all my life, Hammer," she said. "I knew what Makwith was, but I couldn't help myself, whether he was good or bad, right or wrong, I couldn't help myself, I had to ride his trail. And then you came along and it was even worse. As much as I loved Makwith, you did something to me, and that twisted it around even more. I think it was the worst the other day, when I came on you mending that fence. I couldn't love Makwith the way I used to, after all these years, and yet I couldn't leave him, and then, to see you again, like that . . ." She halted, breathing heavily, and when she spoke again, it held a strange, new quietude. "And suddenly, for the first time in my life, now, Hammer . . . I feel whole."

"I haven't much to offer," he said. "But it's all there, down at the Big Dipper, if you want it, Carey."

"I want it," she said. "I want you, Hammer."

Additional Copyright Information

"Town of Twenty Triggers" first appeared in *Lariat Story Magazine* (1/44). Copyright © 1943 by Real Adventures Publishing Co. Copyright © renewed 1971 by Marian R. Savage. Copyright © 2017 by Golden West Literary Agency for restored materials.

"Where Hell's Coyotes Howl" first appeared in *Lariat Story Magazine* (11/45). Copyright © 1945 by Real Adventures Publishing Co. Copyright © renewed 1973 by Marian R. Savage. Copyright © 2017 by Golden West Literary Agency for restored material.

"The Teton Bunch" first appeared under the title "Six-Gun Bride of the Teton Bunch" in *Lariat Story Magazine* (7/47). Copyright © 1947 by Real Adventures Publishing Co. Copyright © renewed 1975 by Marian R. Savage. Copyright © 2017 by Golden West Literary Agency for restored material.

About the Author

Les Savage, Jr. was born in Alhambra, California and grew up in Los Angeles. His first published story was "Bullets and Bullwhips" accepted by the prestigious magazine, Street & Smith's *Western Story*. Almost ninety more magazine stories followed, all set on the American frontier, many of them published in Fiction House magazines such as *Frontier Stories* and *Lariat Story Magazine* where Savage became a superstar with his name on many covers. His first novel, *Treasure of the Brasada*, appeared from Simon & Schuster in 1947. Due to his preference for historical accuracy, Savage often ran into problems with book editors in the 1950s who were concerned about marriages between his protagonists and women of different races—a commonplace on the real frontier but not in much Western fiction in that decade. Savage died young, at thirty-five, from complications arising out of hereditary diabetes and elevated cholesterol. However, as a result of the censorship imposed on many of his works, only now are they being fully restored by returning to the author's original manuscripts. Among Savage's finest Western stories are *Fire Dance at Spider Rock* (Five Star Westerns, 1995), *Medicine Wheel* (Five Star Westerns, 1996),

Coffin Gap (Five Star Westerns, 1997), *Phantoms in the Night* (Five Star Westerns, 1998), *The Bloody Quarter* (Five Star Westerns, 1999), *In the Land of Little Sticks* (Five Star Westerns, 2000), *The Cavan Breed* (Five Star Westerns, 2001), and *Danger Rides the River* (Five Star Westerns, 2002). Much like Stephen Crane before him, while he wrote, the shadow of his imminent death grew longer and longer across his young life, and he knew that if he was going to do it at all, he would have to do it quickly. He did it well, and now that his novels and stories are being restored to what he had intended them to be, his achievement irradiated by his powerful and profoundly sensitive imagination will be with us always, as he had wanted it to be, as he had so rushed against time and mortality that it might be.

Center Point Large Print
600 Brooks Road / PO Box 1
Thorndike, ME 04986-0001 USA

(207) 568-3717

US & Canada:
1 800 929-9108
www.centerpointlargeprint.com